Secret Santa and Other Tales

Tell-Tale Publishing 2nd Annual Horror Anthology

© 2017 Tell-Tale Publishing's 2nd Annual Horror Anthology

Santa's Secret by Marcus Mattern
Funhouse by Patricia Mattern
What Lies Beneath Wraithfall Ruins by Daniel Heaney
Mr. Rumples by George Larson
Shadow Walkers by Elizabeth Alsobrooks
The Long Black Veil and The Night by Ric Wasley

Tell-Tale Publishing Group, LLC
Tucson, AZ 85737

Printed in the United States of America.

Foreword

Oh the horror! The horror!

I've been a fan since my older sister used to wake me up so I could sneak down to watch Creature Feature when I was in elementary school! Funny, I never could seem to get back to sleep. While my main writing focus is the paranormal, my passion for the darker side of the scary spectrum was resurrected while working on Indie horror film, *In The Woods*, helping with the screenplay, writing a novelization, AND having a guest role as "Bar Extra"! That endeavor put Dean Koontz, Stephen King and Justin Cronin into my "Must Read" rotation and convinced me to watch (through my fingers) movies such as *Cabin in the Woods, The Others,* and *Woman in Black.*

Tell-Tale Publishing has an eye for the macabre and for authors who know how to wield a Poe-worthy pen. I've enjoyed being one of the judges in their yearly Halloween talent search (two of the winners are in this edition!). I'm always thrilled to be thrilled by something new in the genre, and this collection fits the bill. Quick, blood-curdling reads to curl up with on a dark night, taken a deadly sip at a time, like a fine, hoarded vintage to savor and appreciate when the nights grow cold and the wind howls. That was the wind wasn't it?

Cheers! Happy reading, and don't forget to leave the nightlight on!

Nancy Gideon, award-winning, bestselling author of the "Touched by Midnight" vampire series and the "By Moonlight" and "House of Terriot" shapeshifter series.

Secret Santa

Marcus Mattern

Winner of Tell-Tale Publishing's Vincent Price Award

Secret Santa

Marcus Mattern

Darren Young dashed out of the boardroom. The shotgun blast and the sight of his boss slumped over the glass conference table weren't even a memory when he flung the door open and sprinted down the hall. Most in the office had already left, and the halls were dark, save for the garish red and green glow of Christmas lights hanging in the hallway.

His head cracked against the sealed exit door as he slammed into it at full speed. The recoil knocked him flat on the ground. Dazed, he rolled over and looked behind him as he pushed to his knees. Linda Baker burst into the hall, her face a mask of terror, then shock, as she got shot in the back and crumpled to the ground.

Scrambling to his feet, he realized the only other exit was back the way he came. Conference and break rooms were on his left, while the cubicle farms were on his right. He dove into an open door and crept under a walled desk somewhere in the middle aisles. More shots followed and he jumped at the reverberating sound of each blast, but when they stopped, and the ringing in his ears subsided, he heard the heavy breathing of other office workers scattered beneath the desks. Then slow, heavy footsteps stung his ears as someone walked into the room.

"He's making a list…"

The haggard voice of a former friend and coworker echoed down the aisles. Someone bolted from under a desk. A shot and a heavy thud followed. A casing ejected from the shotgun.

"Checking it twice…"

He should have been thinking of a better escape plan, but all he could do was wonder what petty negligence he was going to die for.

Burned microwave popcorn? Dead. Free-loading on the potluck? Dead. Not supporting your snotty kid's fundraiser? Dead. Any mistake could be unforgivable. His only chance was to wait for the killer to pass and run the other direction, using the cubicle walls for cover.

"Gonna find out…"

Shit, he's close. But he's also on the other side. A half-wall separated the workspaces to the right and left of Darren, but he had a full wall behind him. All he had to do was wai--

"Who's naughty?"

Darren heard the desk above him creek as his former friend and coworker leapt over the full wall. He felt, before he saw, the shotgun pointing down at him.

"This can end right now," Darren muttered from underneath the desk. He began a slow crawl out of cover, putting his hands up as he rose and turned.

Nick Scoville was dressed in a full Santa suit with Kevlar and combat boots. The blood-speckled white trim of his costume matched his too-wide bloodshot eyes.

"Ho, ho, ho, Darren." Nick lowered the shotgun and pulled a Glock out of his waistband as he stepped down. "You've been *very* naughty this year, but it's not too late for you. You're gonna be Santa's little helper tonight . . . unless you want a lump of coal through your forehead." Nick pressed the barrel of the Glock into Darren's forehead for emphasis and his voice dropped to a growl.

"This is all your fault, after all."

Darren's whole life was supposed to flash before his eyes, but all he could remember is the time he called Nick a pissant. *I don't even know what that word means*, Darren thought, *it just seemed to fit*. Nick had drafted a notification for a network outage and somehow clicked save instead of send. *I mean really, how do you fuck that up?* Darren wasn't very sympathetic.

"Fine. Just. Fine," Darren looked up at Nick, the barrel still pressed against his forehead.

"What do you want?"

Nick's intense focus cracked into a half-smile, and then he smashed Darren's face with a vicious pistol whip.

He giggled. Darren's nose exploded with blood and he fell flat on his ass.

Darren looked up, still feeling betrayed, even if that was silly, given the circumstances. The Glock clattered on the ground beside him as Nick raised the shotgun to his face.

"Now you're gonna be my helper. Point that gun where and how I say. The moment you don't . . . we're both dead. Or maybe just you. I can imagine you fucking this up. Now move."

Darren's trembling hand picked up the gun and gripped it so tight his fingers turned bright red. He took a long time to stand, locking eyes with his captor.

"That's good. Now turn around and start walking."

The static office became a blur of speed as Darren turned away from his former friend and coworker. He could see nothing beyond grey-beige walls, desks, and computers with the occasional flash of color from a Christmas card.

Was everyone gone? He could only hope.

"Walk faster," Nick hissed from behind him.

"You can stop this now," Darren managed to eke out. "Most of the people are already gone. I'm sure everyone will be sorry for what you've been through."

"Nah, they won't be. Not yet, anyway," Nick snickered.

Darren was a terrible negotiator, but talking gave him something to hang onto, a line of communication. With a gun behind his back, it was the only way he could focus.

"Ah-ah. You're missing something. A golden opportunity, if I do say so. An early gift for my new best helper," Nicked said.

Darren's gaze drifted right. A flash of skin shined against a ball of black fabric huddled in a corner underneath a beige desk.

"Point the gun, Darren."

Darren's hand gripped tighter as lifted the pistol toward the desk. A small figure slunk out of the corner and stood, her arms raised.

Mascara streaked down her face with an expression so tense the skin looked stretched over her skull. It was Courtni Hyatt, the new project coordinator.

"That's it. You're holding her now. Same way I'm holding you. Feels kinda nice, right?"

Courtni shuddered with an involuntary sob. Darren tried not to move.

"Now, in case you haven't noticed, there's something special about guns. If you pull the trigger, the only thing they can do is kill someone, or maybe hurt 'em a bit. But if you don't pull it, well . . . they can do just about anything.

"Now tell Courtni to dance."

Darren swallowed a lump in his throat. His hand clenched the gun like a ball of fire, radiating down his arm. Fear reached up from the back of his throat and he spat out the word.

"Dance."

The rhythm in which she moved existed in no song, nor any place or time before that moment. It was a jittering lurch of arms, legs and hips, too in sync with itself to not be dance, but divorced from any sense of time outside of it. Her strained, pleading face stayed fixed on Darren.

"Aw, now see that? That's almost pretty. You made that happen, Darren. Let's see if we can make it a little cuter. Tell her to smile, Darren."

"Smi-" Darren nearly had the word out when he felt her nails raking across his cheek and saw Courtni Wyatt blow past him in a blur and head out the door.

Nick chuckled.

"Tsk, tsk, Darren. You aren't being a very good puppet today. You better start shaping up or I'm gonna throw you out with the other misfit toys. In fact, let me show you what I do with those."

Darren turned back toward Nick. Blood caked on his nose and his gashed cheek. His face flashed with anger. "You know, no matter what, you're gonna die for this, right?"

The PA announcement began to sound throughout the building like the voice of God: "There is an Active Shooter in this building. Please leave through the nearest exit as soon as it is safe to do so."

Nick giggled, "How do you think I made it so far? I made a deal with my death. And he's gonna get everything that's his, right after I get mine." His face fell from that twisted expression of jubilance, melting into something dark and hollow. "I'd rather live as a God for fifteen minutes than spend another second under your heel."

Darren clenched the gun in his hand again. It didn't have to go on for another minute. He could end it right now. Even if he just wounded Nick, the blood loss would still put an end to his rampage.

And as for him? Darren would almost certainly die. *And I've never fired a gun before,* Darren thought. Even if he was willing, it wasn't a choice he could imagine making.

Nick snapped at Darren, breaking his train of thought: "And now that you've shown you're as slow on the trigger as a brain dead reindeer, you can put the fucking gun on the ground. Use that little heal of yours and kick it over."

A jab in the back from the automatic shotgun prodded Darren forward. He raised his hands in the air again, trying to placate his captor, set him at ease for . . . whatever was about to happen.

Darren stepped over the body of Gareth Williams as they approached the exit. He was convulsing in shock--not quite dead, but far from alive. The placid expression behind his glasses and goatee was wide-eyed, suitable for a man approaching a vast, endless nothing.

"See something you like?" Nick snarled. Darren picked up the pace without any further prompt. His hands clasped his aching ears as a shot from the Glock went off behind him. He glanced back to see a hole in Gareth's temple, and the blank stare of death on his face.

"Mercy," Nick whispered as he placed the Glock back in his waistband. He had a curious sense of justice. The only rule was that he made the rules.

Darren walked down the hall, not sure whether to shield his eyes as they passed the conference room on the left. In the end, he needed to know how many more had been shot down.

His boss, Terry Hagen was the only body he saw in the room as they walked around Lin Baker, face down in the middle of the hall. *Fewer than I thought*, Darren realized as they passed the conference room. A tiny hope began to swell inside him for those that still lived.

Maybe Lisa's safe at home, he thought. Darren had never found an appropriate way of telling her how she made him smile. He could imagine her accepting or rejecting his advances because he was her boss, but it could never be a non-issue. *Maybe when I switch companies*, he always told himself. He had sworn to find another job at the start of the new year.

He made himself the same promise last year, too.

"Where are we going?" he whispered over his shoulder. The quiet became uncomfortable as Darren remembered the gun pointed at his back.

"To celebrate," Nick said with a grin. "Second door on your left."

***

The Human Resources department was abandoned, leaving only the yellow glow of an artificial Christmas tree in the corner.

Darren had almost breathed a sigh of relief when his eyes fixed on a large black duffel bag laying at the foot of the tree.

"My little elves have been busy," Nick said with a nervous chuckle.

Darren blanched. "Who else is here?"

"Oh. You don't know that about Santas," Nick said, salivating over the words. "We got elves all over. All waiting to drop their big boy balls and become Santas. Till then, they help us out. My little workshop churned out a nice big present."

Nick approached Darren's shoulder and leaned in. The stench of eggnog and whiskey bloomed off his rotting teeth. His eyes flared wide and flickered with anticipation.

"My little elves tell me you've been wishing for this all year."

Darren sighed. His shaking legs caved and he crashed to his knees. He put a hand on the bag before even looking for the zipper.

It was warm.

"Oh, it's too late for guessing, Darren. It's the last Christmas for you and me. You have to open it."

The smell began pouring out as soon as the zipper slid an inch. The inside was rancid and Darren gagged from the wave of stench as the bag slid open. He covered his mouth and looked down

Glistening on the inside were the auburn-haired head and entrails of Lisa Foley.

"You know, it was really satisfying to take her apart and scrutinize every piece. I know it's what she did to you and me."

Nick poked the back of Darren's head for emphasis as he said, "Now grab a handful of sausage, it's time to string her up."

Darren half-closed his eyes and tried to breathe through his mouth as he gathered the small intestines in his arms and found a dangling end, still attached to a piece of Lisa's stomach. It hooked onto the branches at the bottom of the tree, and Darren began wrapping the outside. He had rounded the tree three times and still had length to spare when Nick chimed in.

"That's good enough for now. The Grinches are gonna be here soon. Why don't you reach in the bag and put a star on top. It's not really a Christmas tree without a star, is it?"

Darren dropped the rest of Lisa Foley's intestines and convulsed with sobs. He fell to his knees and covered his face with bloodied hands.

"Oh, you were sweet on her, were ya? Well guess what, there's room enough on the top for your fat head if you'd rather. Otherwise, I'd get your grubby fucking hands around her neck right now."

Nick fired into the air, and a deafening wave of sound shook Darren to attention. He looked back at Nick with acute awareness and the shotgun barrel burned his skin as Nick pushed him back toward the bag.

Darren reached in and grabbed her slack-jawed skull. It was the first time he'd ever touched her skin. Crying, but not blinking, he took great care raising her head to the top. The inside of the neck had been hollowed out and he let its weight rest on the tree, making a snug fit.

A piece of branch stuck through her mouth and her eyes were frozen open.

Nick smiled with approval. "Beautiful. Never let anyone tell you office work is not creative. Now crawl on the fucking ground until you reach the door."

Darren thought about bolting again, but remembered the body of Gareth Williams, shot in the back in the cubicle office. His bloody hands left tracks on the ground as he pawed along the coarse, mottled-grey carpet. The twenty-foot distance to the door felt interminable, yet every moment was a blur, catapulting him into the next with unrelenting force.

"You know no one's ever gonna trust you after this," Nick said. "It doesn't matter how desperate the situation is, in their eyes you're already tainted. It's not really your fault though. You do what you do because you've got a gun to your head. Most days it's called mortgage. Today it's called 12-gauge, Smith and Wesson."

Nick grabbed Darren by the hair from behind and pulled him to his feet, "Now seeing as you're so used to it, I'm gonna let the cops point at you too. And you're gonna give me your life for Christmas just like Jesus himself, or I'm gonna take it."

Nick grabbed the collar on the back of Darren's shirt and pressed the gun barrel into his back. "Now open the fucking door."

Darren's trembling hand became firm as he reached the door handle. The mechanical sound of the lock echoed in his mind as the door opened.

The empty hall was dark and silent as the pair stepped through. Darren kept his hands raised. A noxious cloud of heavy breaths emanated from behind him.

"Where are we going?" he asked as they turned left. Somehow not knowing was worse than what he'd just been through.

Nick's speech was slurred with drool, "The only thing this feast is missing is a Christmas Ham. We're going on a late night pork run. Keep your eyes open for any pigs."

Darren gulped. As they walked, he focused on his and Nick's footsteps. In desperation, his ears searched for more.

He opened one of the two large doors in front of him and entered a T-junction with a larger hallway and more garish decorations. Large, plastic candy canes and Santa posters coated the walls, lit by a rainbow-glow of multicolored lights and silver garland. A matching set of double doors stood across from them.

"Where-" Darren's question was cut short as nick whipped him in the back of the head with the barrel of the shotgun.

"Do I look like I fuckin' know, just pick a direction!" Nick screamed, spraying spittle on the back of Darren's head. One of the large doors across from them swung open and a SWAT team member sprang out.

The blast from Nick's shotgun sprayed her uncovered face with buckshot and she was blown back behind the door, her helmet and Kevlar vest untouched.

Darren, ears ringing, grabbed Nick's arm with both hands and heaved his shoulder up into his elbow. The shotgun dropped to the ground as Nick's arm snapped backward with a wet pop.

Darren dove forward and cradled the shotgun with both arms like the child he never had. He looked back and saw Nick writhing on the ground, desperate to put his arm back in place.

Springing to his feet, Darren hurled the butt of the shotgun at Nick's face and collapsed his weight into the attack. He heard a sickening crunch as Nick's cheek bone collapsed and he fell to his knees. Adrenaline jolted him to his feet, and he smashed Nick's face over and over. Lost in desperate rage, he didn't realize the door behind them had opened until after he fell.

A wave of numb wetness painted his back. The SWAT officer wasn't alone, three others raced to surround them on all sides. Darren mustered what strength he had left to look behind his back. A tall, broad-shouldered man in full armor was radioing back, "Santa is down! Repeat, Santa is down!"

Darren's eyes welled with tears as he realized he wouldn't survive. The blood was pouring out his chest, pooling up to his face. His weary eyes searched for answers and found Nick. The right half of his face was crushed with the eye hanging out of its socket. And yet the other side, beaten bloody, held a wry half-smile.

"I had to prove it, you know. That I wasn't a pissant," he said with grim satisfaction.

Darren spoke though a voice choked with blood. "Of all the ways you could have chosen . . ." Darren's gaze burned into Nick's mangled two-face. His body writhed with hated and still he laid, unable to move. "What the fuck, Nick?"

"I loved you, Darren," he said, tears dripping down his hanging eye. "And you didn't even know I existed unless I managed to piss you off!" Nick's face tensed with an agony his physical wounds could not approach.

"So I listened to the little voice inside of me, the one that never leaves. It tells me I can *have* more. I *deserve* more. It's a secret little Santa inside everybody and all it ever asks you to do is say 'yes.'"

Nick coughed up blood as the stamping sound of many more officers echoed from up the hall. Darren was starting to pass out when he heard Nick dragging himself forward with his good arm. The Christmas icon winced as he dragged his broken arm behind him and slowed as he came within reach. A rough hand reached out and clutched Darren's chin.

"King for a day, it told me!" Nick's eyes shined with an unholy gleam. "Fifteen minutes of fame. No one will ever look at you the same way again."

Nick let go of Darren and lowered his eyes in a disarming display of shame as he whispered "And I had to . . ." Nick gripped Darren's collar and pulled, drawing even closer with heavy, liquor-filled breaths. The wet heat washed over Darren's face.

"I know it seems bad," Nick whispered, "But those girls in the office just couldn't have loved you like I can."

Nick leaned into to Darren and gave his frozen face a kiss with thick, wet lips.

"And I'm *somebody* to you," he whispered. "And no matter how much you hate me and wish I never existed, I do now. And I'll love you no matter how much you hurt me back."

"You are under arrest!" cried a heavy-set man in a police uniform.

Darren saw an officer come down from behind Nick and cuff his bent-back arm to the other as he cried out in pain.

"You have the right to remain silent!"

Another officer was pinning Darren's arms behind and cuffing them, but he could barely feel it.

"Anything you say can and will be used against you!"

All of his senses were slipping away, like a leased car towed for a lapse in payments. His body, not yet gone, was already not his.

"I'm okay now," Nick assured Darren as he entered a final lapse in consciousness. "There's nothing worse than being nothing."

The Long Black Veil

Ric Wasley

The Long Black Veil

Ric Wasley

There is a legend in the hills of Appalachia of a mysterious veiled woman who walks the shadowy forests and lonely places in search of her lost lover. The legend, told in both story and song, is said to hearken back to events long forgotten and dark secrets kept within the hills and hollows of the old places. No one is quite sure where these rumors and legends actually originated or what was the real story behind them, but here is what might have happened...

The moon has just risen, and I can now make out the narrow dirt path winding up from the village like a ribbon of silver.

There will be a frost tonight; I can smell it in the air. The leaves are almost gone from the trees, and it won't be long until the first snowfall blankets the valley. There's already a touch of ice rime on the tops of the hills that march upward until they join the Great Smokies on the Tennessee side. I should really whistle up the dogs and get on up to hills to see if I can't bag a buck before the snow settles into the high passes.

Ol' Marcus down at the dry goods store claims it's gonna be a hard winter. *Humph*–it can't be no harder than any of those winters spent freezing in Virginia or in the cold muddy trenches outside of Richmond.

That's where Captain Denby lost his leg, and I almost lost my life. When the preachers talk about how 'no greater love hath a man for his friends than he lay down his life,' I reckon they must be talkin' about my captain and boyhood friend, Clayton Danby. What's more, on the day he did it, I think he knew I'd been in love with Miss Amanda–the woman who became his wife–since the first day we saw her ten years ago.

Her family had just moved to town, and we were still a pair of boys dreaming of becoming men.

In those days, we challenged each other to foot races, wrestling matches, and even made swords out of fence pickets so we could pretend we were pirates or knights bent on rescuing some fair damsel. The Sunday we saw Miss Amanda Harrington standing like a golden princess on the church steps, we both fell in love with her. Me and Clay spent the next six years doing every fool thing we could think of trying to impress her. For her part, she flirted and smiled at the both us. In general, she made us feel like we were kings of the county and that she loved us above all of her other beaus. But even though I always felt the looks she gave me lingered longer and the smiles in my direction were just a bit brighter than those she bestowed upon Clay, all three of us knew in the end who she'd marry. He was a Denby, and I was only a Hackett. And Miss Amanda Harrington from Charlotte wasn't gonna marry no son of a hardscrabble farmer.

One week before the wedding, I was out hunting when I heard a horse coming up behind me. At first, I was angry someone was gonna scare off the fox I'd been trailing, but when a big chestnut mare nosed through the branches, and I saw Miss Amanda's eyes all green and gold twinkling back at me, I forgot all about that fox. I'll tell you true, if she had asked me to run off with her that day, I would have jumped through hoops for her and never looked back. But she wasn't coming to tell me that–she was coming to say goodbye. She was marrying Clay, and that was the way things had to be. But just when I was thinking I might as well fill my pockets with rocks and jump into the creek, she took both of my rough hands in her tiny soft ones and looked at me with this sad, little look that broke my heart and made it race all at the same time.

"Silas," she said to me. "I had to come and see you one last time to tell you that even though we can't be together, I love you. I always have and I always will." Then she threw her arms around me and kissed my lips with a kiss that I'd dream of every night for four years hence.

For the next week, I thought about stealing her away. By the day of the wedding, I had set my mind that when the preacher said, "And if there is any man here who knows why this couple can not be joined in holy matrimony, let him speak now or forever hold his peace…" I was gonna jump up and scream, "Yes! Because she loves me." And I would have been in a very good position to snatch her hand out of Clay's, because I was the best man.

Sadly, that was the one thing I couldn't do. It was my duty to stand next to my best friend and hand him the ring that would take from me forever the only woman I'd ever love.

That night, I left the wedding feast early, took a jug of 40-rod, and drank until I passed out underneath the pine trees. When I finally came to the next day, I decided to pack up and light out over the mountains for the west. Maybe I'd head on down to Memphis and take a steamboat for New Orleans. But before I'd ridden a mile, I met Clay riding the other way to find me. He was in high state and grinning from ear to ear.

"Silas," he said to me, "it's finally happened. Our boys have fired on the Federals at Fort Sumter. It's gonna be war!" He let out this big whoop and said, "My pa has thrown in the money to raise a company of volunteers from the county. I'm gonna be the captain, and I want you to be my sergeant." He looked at me–his face all red and happy as if he didn't have a care in the world or hadn't been married but a day to the most beautiful woman on God's green earth. "What do you say old friend—will you march with me?"

So Clayton Denby and Silas Hackett marched off to war. Four years later, the man who I envied every day of my life pushed me out of harm's way and took a blast of grape shot that had been meant for me.

Now, I was waiting in the old village burying ground above the town on this cold, moonlit night for the sweetest kisses I had ever known. Those of Amanda Harrington Denby—my best friend's wife.

* * * *

When the collection of over-worked and half-drunk surgeons in what passed for a field hospital on that bloody butcher's ground got through with Clay, one leg was gone and the other was mostly useless. That's how I carried him home to his bride who'd spent no more than a month with him over the past four years.

When I helped untie him from his horse and carry him upstairs, I thought it was good he did all that dancing at his wedding, 'cause he wasn't never gonna dance again.

I don't know what I mumbled to Amanda, but I couldn't bear the sight of her face as she looked at what war had done to her brave cavalier. I was feeling no end of shame for loving her even at that moment—until I stumbled down the stairs to my horse and didn't stop riding 'til I hit the tavern in town. Bad liquor and bad judgment was always my undoing.

I should have kept my hand off the jug and my mouth closed, but I was of a mind to do neither. So when the overblown braggart at the end of the bar started in about how we should have never surrendered and how those that did shamed the "Cause" and the Confederacy, I up and asked him what regiment he'd served with.

Said he, "I'm a Captain of the Home Guard and I outrank you Sergeant, so just you close your capitulatin' mouth and say 'Sir' the next time you address me."

"Your rank don't count for nothin' with men that done the real fighting and dying, you puffed up, swill-guzzling son-of-a-bitch!"

Well, up he came, roaring at me screaming and hollering, but I laid him out on the barroom floor with one good blow to his fat gut.

While he laid there gasping like a gaffed catfish, I said, "And if I ever hear you bad-mouthing a North Carolina fighting man again, I'm gonna kill you."

That was a mistake.

* * * *

The night is growing colder, and the wind is whistling through the trees and moaning like a dying man on a battlefield. But the moon is fully up now, and bits of clouds like dirty grey cotton blow across it, making patterns and shapes on the stone slabs all around me. I'm sitting on one while I wait for her. It's cold, but it doesn't bother me. Maybe that's because thinking about her crowds every other thought out of my mind.

I can see a light now. It's starting up the path from the far side of town where the main street meets the pike road that passes by the pastureland and orchards of the big farms. Farms big enough to be plantations in the low counties. Big acre farms with big, beautiful houses like Tall Pines–the Denby place.

* * * *

I didn't want to call on Clay and Amanda. In fact, all I wanted to do was to light out for the mountains and the west. I wanted to forget about the war and ever loving a girl with green eyes and honey-golden hair. But being born and raised in a place and owing a man your life puts a body under certain obligations. Before I could leave, I had to go and pay my respects to my best friend and his wife.

As I rode up the long, tree-lined drive that led up to the main house, I could see Clay from a long way off. He was on the porch, and when I got closer, I saw he was sitting in a wicker chair contraption with wheels that could be dragged from place to place.

I got off my horse, and my boot heels made hollow sounds as I walked up the warped, peeling pine boards of the porch steps. Tall Pines had been the showplace of the county before the war, but now it had fallen on hard times. Just like the man who owned it.

Clay stuck out his right hand and smiled, but there was no warmth behind it. He was like a broken bucket that the water had leaked out of.

"I hope you'll forgive me for not getting up, Silas. I seem to find that it's not worth the effort these days."

I tried to smile, but mine was like his–just a movement of the mouth with no warmth behind it.

"How you doing, Clay?" I asked, but I could see with my own eyes. His face was puffy, and his skin had a saggy, grey look. One leg of his pants was tucked up underneath him while the other leg stuck straight out.

"Well, I'll tell you old friend, I think that my dancing days are over." Neither of us laughed. "So maybe if the balls and parties ever start up again, you could do your old captain one last favor and squire Miss Amanda around the dance floor for me, eh, Silas?"

"You know, I ain't no great shakes at dancing, Clay, I…"

I never got to finish my sentence because at that moment the front door opened, and Amanda Harrington Denby stepped onto the porch. She looked pale, as if she hadn't been sleeping well, but she was still the most beautiful woman I'd ever seen.

"Silas," she said with real warmth, "it's been too long since we've seen you at Tall Pines." She stood up on tiptoes and kissed me on the cheek. She smelled like roses and honeysuckle. "And you'll stay for dinner, isn't that right, Clayton?"

"Thank you kindly, Miss Amanda, but I got places I gotta get going to, and I'm not sure that …"

"Now don't make me make this an order, Sergeant Hackett." Clay smiled, but there were cold places behind the smile where the dead, mangled and soulless waited for the final bugle blast that would send them all marching to hell.

I saw that behind Amanda's own gracious smile, her eyes were pleading with me.

"All right Captain," I finally nodded, "you got yourself a dinner guest."

* * * *

All though dinner Clay left most of his food untouched but continued to punish the crystal decanter of hundred-proof sippin' whiskey. Amanda tried to draw him into conversation, but as the night wore on and the candles burned down, his answers became shorter and bitterer until his head fell forward and his chin rested on his chest.

I glanced over at Amanda. She stared at the table, a handkerchief twisted in her hands and twin tears rolling down her cheeks. I stood up, walked up to her, and awkwardly patted her on the shoulder. She stood up, took my hand, and led me into the parlor.

As soon as she swung the double doors closed, she threw herself into my arms and buried her face in my shirt. "Oh, Silas, it gets worse every night. He's hurting so, and I don't know what to do to make it better."

We stood like that for a long time. She told me about Clay and what being crippled was doing to him and how helpless she felt. I told her I felt the same way and wished I could do something to help them both, and then I told her I was leaving for the west at sun-up the next day.

She looked up at me with a strange expression on her face. After a long time, she said, "Silas, do you still love me?"

I wasn't expecting that and got so tongue tied that I could only nod.

"Then will you do something for me?"

"Anything."

"Very well. Then I want you to leave now. But later tonight after I've helped Clayton up to bed, I want you to return. My bedroom fronts on the second floor balcony. I'll be waiting for you."

All the way back to town my face burned, and my heart beat like a drummer's muster call. I stopped into the tavern and ordered a whiskey, but when I thought about her lips, I put it back down on the bar, untasted.

"What's this–is our fightin' soldier-boy getting' scared of whiskey now as well as the Yankees?"

I looked up. The Home Guard captain's big belly pushed up against the bar. "I told you once before, Mumford, that the next time I heard you bad-mouthing our fightin' men, I was gonna put a bullet through your fat gut."

A half-dozen veterans of our company who were sitting at a table in the corner applauded and raised their glasses to me.

Mumford's face became a mottled red, and as I turned and walked out of the tavern he shouted, "Well, just you try it, boy! I'll be waiting on you. Any place–any time!"

I didn't answer because I had more important things than takin' up the challenge of a loudmouth drunkard.

But later that night, someone else did. Because as Captain Mumford stepped out of the Tavern, one shot rang out, and he fell, dead, face first into the street.

* * * *

It's odd how I feel the wind but not the cold. Or if I do feel it, I don't seem to care.

I hear a screech owl in the distance, but I don't care about that either.

I only care about one thing.

I can see it more clearly now. It is most definitely a light–a lantern. I can't make out a figure, but I already know who's carrying it: Amanda.

* * * *

The sheriff caught up with me on the mountain road. He said, "I got a writ for you, Hackett, and it charges you with murder in the first degree."

* * * *

By the time we got back to town, it was spitting a cold, bone chillin' rain. As we started down the main street, I twisted my head back to see the top of the ridge that wound over to the Smokies coated with a powdering of white. "Guess there'll be no making it through the high pass tonight," I told myself. At the same time, I tried not to think about the fact that this was the closest I might ever get to making it over those mountains.

I turned back and looked toward town again. Small knots of people were gathering on the stone curbs and wooden boardwalks in front of the stores. It was plain from the looks on their faces they didn't think I'd be crossing the mountains either.

The county sheriff, Tom Davis, wasn't a bad sort and tried to help me as much as he could within the confines of the law. His wife was a good cook, and every night I was in that jail cell, she made sure I had a hot meal and even chicken fricassee on Sunday. Between her and the wives and sisters of the veterans of my old company, I must have got sent at least a dozen pies and pastry cakes. But when I tried to enjoy them from behind the black-iron bars of that county cage, the sweet icing turned to paste and the cake as dry and dusty as plaster.

Every day I waited for Amanda to come, but as the weeks dragged on and my trial approached, I began to understand why she couldn't. She was Amanda Harrington Denby, and I was still the son of a hardscrabble farmer.

'Course that wasn't the real reason–but I didn't find that out until the day of the trial.

* * * *

"Silas Whitcomb Hackett, you are hereby charged that on the 2nd day of December in the year of our Lord Eighteen Hundred and Sixty-Five, you did deliberately and, with malice aforethought, murder one Henry Mumford, acting captain in the Home Guard of Waynesville, North Carolina. How plead you, Mr. Hackett?"

I stood up in the witness box and wiped my damp palms on my pants. "Not guilty, your honor, upon my soul."

"We shall see about that, Mr. Hackett–we shall see."

The judge's gavel slammed down upon the bench like the cracking sound that the trap door on the gallows makes when the lever is sprung—the terrible and final sound it makes as the condemned man falls through it for six feet or so until the snap of his neck echo's in his ears for eternity.

"The county prosecutor may call his first witness."

I watched numbly as the tavern keeper shambled up to the front of the courtroom and stood opposite me in the witness box.

"Mr. Joseph Barnaby, do you recall seeing and/or hearing an argument take place between the accused and the late Captain Mumford?"

Barnaby's eyes wouldn't meet mine but he answered up right smart enough. "Yes, sir, I surely do."

Jesiah Sloan, the prosecutor was a ferret-eyed, dried up little man with a voice like a broken reed in the wind. But he piled on his evidence against me just fine.

"And did you, Mr. Barnaby, hear the accused, one Silas Hackett, threaten Henry Mumford with grave bodily harm?"

"Yes, sir, Silas told Captain Mumford that if he ever heard him bad-mouthin' North Carolina fightin' boys again, he was gonna kill him dead."

"And did he not repeat this threat on the very night that poor Captain Mumford was most foully murdered?"

"Yes, sir, he did."

"And was the captain not shot through the chest just two hours later as he emerged from your tavern?"

"Yes, sir. By one single shot, right through the heart. And that's a fact!"

The thin lawyer put his hands in his pockets and rocked back and forth on his heels as if considering the testimony. "Yes, a single shot–right through the heart. Quite a feat of marksmanship wouldn't you say so, Mr. Barnaby?"

"Yup, I reckon so."

"And what sort of man would have the training and skill to make such a shot?" He turned to the jury, and they stared back at him, waiting for the conclusion they all knew was coming. "Do you think perhaps a … soldier?" He whirled and pointed at me. "And what has been your occupation for the past four years, Mr. Hackett?"

I hardly felt it was worth the breath answering, but I finally did. "You know damn well, Mr. Sloan, I been fighting with my regiment for the Cause."

"And in your capacity as…" He picked up a piece of paper and made a great show of reading what he already knew. "As—yes, here it is—First Sergeant of the Waynesville Volunteers, was it your duty to instruct your men in marksmanship, Sergeant?"

"Yes, sir, and my privilege."

"And would you say that you were an accurate shot, Sergeant Hackett?"

I waited a moment before I answered. "I was a dead shot."

* * * *

My lawyer was some kid who'd got in one year of law school before he was conscripted. He was no match for Sloan. But I still had one ace up my sleeve because there was one person who knew I wasn't within ten miles of that tavern when Mumford was killed, and she was walking up to the witness box with small, dainty steps.

"Mrs. Denby," Sloan began, "I know you to be a good, honest, and truthful woman with a family and reputation beyond reproach, so I will ask you, was the accused, one Silas Hackett at your home on the night in question?"

Amanda cast me a quick glance and answered, "Yes, Mr. Sloan, he was our guest for dinner."

"And was there anyone else present at the dinner other than you and your husband, Captain Denby?" Sloan flashed Clay an ingratiating smile, but Clayton just stared through him at his wife.

"No, sir–all of our folk ran off or left when we had no money to pay them for their service."

"A pity," Sloan remarked perfunctorily. "So then the only ones to see Mr. Hackett leave were you and your husband?"

Amanda shook her head, her eyes fixed on the floor. "No. My husband–Captain Denby, he…he fell asleep."

There was complete silence in the courtroom. I could hear the clock ticking behind the judge as if it were counting down the minutes of my life. I knew what the next question would be and, at that moment, I didn't know how I wanted her to answer it.

"Mrs. Denby, would you please tell the court at what time Mr. Hackett left your home?"

"It…it was sometime after ten o'clock."

"And Mr. Hackett was seen drinking in the tavern at ten-thirty and left around eleven." Sloan stroked his chin. "And poor Captain Mumford was shot through the heart as he left the tavern at eleven-thirty."

Amanda twisted her handkerchief and didn't raise her eyes.

Sloan walked around until he stood directly in front of the witness box. "Now, Mrs. Denby, I have a very delicate but very important question to ask you. Did Mr. Hackett return for any reason whatsoever that night?"

Clay's eyes burned like twin black coals as he gripped the handles of his wheelchair.

Finally Amanda looked up, and her eyes met mine. They sparked with unshed tears. "No."

* * * *

The sound of a key turning in the lock of my cell forced my eyes back from where they'd been staring trough the single window to the mountains beyond the town.

"You got a visitor, son, but you'd best make it quick if you want to have the parson read you some words of comfort before you step off into eternity."

Eternity–that was some thought. I guess the jailor, though, in his own way, was trying to put the best face on it.

I got up from my straw tick cot and combed my hair out of my eyes with my hands. It was hard to do because the manacles kept getting in the way.

The door to my cell clanked open, and Mrs. Amanda Harrington Denby walked into my cell.

She didn't speak until the jailor locked the door and moved off down the hallway. When she heard the outer door close, she threw herself into my arms.

"Silas! Oh, my love, how you must hate me!"

"I could never hate you Amanda. All I could ever do was love you."

"Then I hate myself! But what could I do? I couldn't tell the world that while Mr. Mumford was being murdered, I was opening my bedchamber door to you," she looked up at me, eyes wet with unshed tears, "the man that I realized too late that I would always love."

She put her head down on the coarse homespun cotton of my shirt and wept.

I wrapped my arms around her as far as the chain would permit and held her awkwardly. I'd never have time to get used to the feeling of her in my arms.

"You did the right thing, Amanda. This is truly better for me than destroying whatever is left of the life of my best friend, the man who gave up so much of his life for mine. Even if you'd spoken up for me, I couldn't have lived with myself anyway. If Clay hadn't killed me, I'd have blown my own brains out."

"But there was another reason that I couldn't speak. The most important one of all."

I looked at her. No…it couldn't be.

"I'm going to have a baby."

My knees gave way, and I sat down on the bunk.

"Lord have mercy! And is it…"

She nodded. "I'm not sure whether Clayton can beget a child any more. But when I told him, he was so proud. Maybe he can stop seeing himself as merely a cripple."

I took a deep breath. Perhaps this was the way I finally got to pay back for my life, for my love–everything.

She clutched my hands. "But this doesn't mean that I will ever stop loving you–ever!"

"I'm glad Amanda, 'cause that will be a comfort to me when I take that final step into eternity." I managed to smile at her.

"No!"

I stepped back and looked at her.

"You don't have to die, Silas. I won't let you die!"

I heard a creak and a scrape as the outer door opened. The jailor was coming back.

"Quick!" she hissed, "Take this."

She had thrust her kerchief into my hands. Wrapped up in it were a small two-shot Derringer and a folding clasp knife.

"The knife is razor sharp, it can cut through the hangman's rope, and the pistol will keep them off you until you can escape. Run to the livery stable–there will be a horse waiting, and then ride to the old Jessup place and hide there until sunset."

We could hear the jailor's footsteps. "Meet me at nightfall in the old churchyard above the town. I will come to you there, and we shall somehow decide what is best for all of us in this world of twists and turns."

She stepped away from me as the jailor turned the corner and unlocked the cell door. She folded her hands, stepped through the door, and didn't look back.

* * * *

It all worked out just the way Amanda said it would.

While the preacher read the words to me, I slipped the knife down from my sleeve and sawed through the slack in the rope. I was afraid I hadn't sufficient time to get through enough of it to ensure it would break under my weight.

Fortunately for me, the preacher was a windy, old bird. By the time he'd finished, I'd cut halfway through. Now I was still a mite nervous because I've never been what you'd call a heavy feller, but although I got one hell of a jolt, and my neck still hurts, the rope parted, and I made it to the stable and away before any of them had recovered their wits.

* * * *

Now here I sit, up high on the hilltop overlooking the town, waiting in the old churchyard just like she asked me to. It seems as if I've been waiting here for years and years. Just sitting on one of the old gravestones and waiting for her.

My Amanda.

It's funny how I don't seem to care about much. I don't feel cold or hungry or much of anything. The only thing I feel is a longing to hold her in my arms once more.

Soon.

There she is. I can see her quite clearly now. She's holding the lantern high–looking for me.

"Over here, Amanda! Over by the big oak tree. I'm sitting here on the gravestone underneath the tree and I'm waiting for you, just like I promised."

She sees me now and runs toward me. Her hair is undone, and it flies in the wind.

Now she is here with me. I throw my arms around her, and I can smell the scent of honeysuckle and roses in her hair once more.

Her face is wet; she's been crying. She is so beautiful, but she looks tired. There are tiny lines around her mouth and a few of the strands of her long, golden hair are tipped with grey. I never noticed that before. This has been very hard on her.

But no matter. We are together now, and that's all that matters. I hold her tightly–she feels so light and insubstantial in my arms, as though she is made of gossamer.

She is speaking to me. I drink in each word.

"Silas! Oh, Silas! I thought that with time I'd forget you, but I don't. Your memory grows stronger in my heart each year."

"Amanda, what's wrong? Why are you crying? Don't cry, my love, we're together and that is everything."

"Can you ever forgive me?"

She has sunk to her knees and holds the cold stone grave marker as if it were a lover.

"Amanda, what is wrong? Why won't you look at me?"

But she does not. She clutches the stone and weeps as if her heart is broken for all time.

"I am responsible for your death. You gave me a child, and I gave you death. What did you think when you realized that the blade of the knife I gave you had been purposely dulled so that the rope could not be cut."

"No, Amanda, you don't know what you're saying."

She leans her face against the stone and kisses it. "But please believe me, Silas; I loved you 'til the end and with all of my heart. I knew there was no place we could run to from honor and duty, from my husband, your friend and…our child. I hoped and prayed the knife would give you hope and solace. Perhaps you could even imagine it cutting you free and, in your final moments, a dream of us being together."

She puts her head into her hands and pulls the long black veil down over her face.

She weeps softly, but the sobs sound muted to me now. I try to pat her shoulder, tell her that I understand, but my hand is like smoke, and it drifts away on the wind.

I kneel down beside her and look at the words written on the stone.

Silas Whitcomb Hackett–Sergeant and Veteran of Waynesville Volunteers - E Company

Born: September 10, 1843
Died: January 21, 1866
Erected in loving memory by
Mrs. Amanda Harrington Denby

I drift away on the wailing wind and finally cross over the mountains.

33

Funhouse

P. Mattern

Funhouse
P. Mattern

"Daryl Finch, you chicken shit, you either go with us or I'll give you an Indian rope burn," Flip threatened.

It was no idle threat. Phillippa, Daryl's sister, who preferred to be called by her nickname 'Flip' was notorious for her ability to administer that particular form of childhood torture and peer punishment

Flip, always a tomboy and already a head taller than Daryl, had been a Daddy's girl and had taken it hard when their Dad died suddenly seven months earlier. As a result, their beleaguered mother, already eight months pregnant when her husband died, had been called to their elementary school repeatedly to discuss Flip's bullying behavior.

Daryl, Flip and their next door neighbors, Tracey Prescott, Jr. and his little sister Eva, were at the carnival with their mothers. Daryl and Flip's mother was wearing a tummy pac with their youngest sibling, 6 month old Randy, in it.

Tracey, big for his age and a 6th grader was the oldest. His sister Eva was in the same 4th grade class as Flip.

Daryl had been held back a year, so he was a fifth grader for the second time. It bothered him because it meant that he and Tracey wouldn't ever be in the same class again.

Tracey and Eva's mother was their own mother's best friend, although judging by appearances the two women were polar opposites.

Mrs. Prescott was glamorous for a small town mom, and Daryl thought that she was beautiful. His crush on Tracey's mom was one of his deepest, darkest secrets and one that he kept to himself.

Daryl shaded his eyes with his hand from the harsh noonday sun and looked over to where their mothers were sitting under a tree at a picnic table, talking. Both the mothers had agreed that unless they all went into the Fun House together, no one could.

Daryl glanced back at the entrance to the Fun House, and his stomach did a flip flop again. There was something foreboding about the entrance, a giant gaping mouth with red clown lips and rows of sharp jagged teeth hanging down.

It didn't look fun to him. Just scary.

His friend Tracey put a hand on Daryl's shoulder.

"It's just a bunch of fun house mirrors," he said, "And clowns jumping out at you. It's no big deal. You can stick with me if you want."

Daryl looked around the semi-circle of expectant faces around him, then down at the youngest, Eva.

"Don't be scared, Daryl," she said, a babyish lisp in her voice, "I'm not!"

That decided it.

"Okay," he said.

Flip stopped scowling at him and Tracey ran over to get the ticket money from their moms, kicking up dust as he trotted back. It had been a dry summer, and it was 90 degrees today.

Suddenly the cool darkness inside the Fun House seemed more appealing.

After the kids bought their tickets, they walked up the short path. There was a large rotating circle that looked like the inside of a barrel just inside the entrance that you were supposed to skip across quickly enough not to lose your footing. Determined to be first to make up for his earlier reluctance, Daryl stepped in and immediately lost his balance. To the amusement of the others he got stuck on his butt in the portal, with his legs getting flipped over his head.

He was so disoriented he stayed there for over a full minute, the sound of raucous laughter ringing in his ears. A black couple that was passing by stopped to stare and chuckle at the chubby white kid being folded over repeatedly by the rotation of the tunnel entrance.

Finally with the sheer strength of self-disgust, Daryl scrambled up and leapt into the dark interior, free of the cylinder. After he was in, Tracey, Flip and even little Eva jumped into the interior just fine.

There was a cloying darkness in front of them, the clammy walls on either side made up to look like the walls of a cavern. Indirect lighting by artificial torches lit up the cavern ceiling, which was painted in lurid colors, depicting a scene of horned devils with waving tails peering down at them hungrily.

"Cool," Tracey said, staring upward.

They rounded one blind curve, activating a mechanical bat that flew directly above them, practically parting Trace's hair. Eva shrieked and then giggled.

As they rounded a second blind curve, someone dressed in a clown costume jumped at them from an alcove. Even Flip shrieked.

"Not real," Tracey told them. Sure enough, the life-sized clown that had seemed alive retreated back jerkily into a deep alcove after a few seconds.

Daryl found himself beginning to relax. Up ahead all of them gleamed an oasis of bright light, and they moved toward it eagerly.

Once there, they found themselves in a room that was roughly octagonal, with mirrors on all sides, large and small, including some fanning out from the center of the ceiling above their heads.

The Hall of Mirrors was beautiful and bizarre at the same time.

There were mirrors that made all of them look fat, and others in which they appeared tall and thin.

All of them were laughing. Flip discovered one that distorted their cheeks until they looked like a bunch of chipmunks. They took turns standing in front of each of them to check out the humorous effects.

The closer they got to the largest mirror at the very end of the long room the more interesting their reflections got. One mirror made them all look like clowns, with huge rubbery lips and oversized gloved hands and comically long feet.

One made them look like dinosaurs. Tracey and Daryl had a discussion trying to figure out how they could possible do that, and decided that there must be some sort of projector behind the mirror that added the dinosaur bodies and tails accurately, based on height.

The visual effects were amazing.

"Look! I'm a queen," Eva exclaimed, standing in front of one of the last mirrors.

In front of her she saw reflected a flattering likeness that didn't seem quite right. The small figure DID look like her, blonde curly hair and bangs cut just a little too short because her mom didn't want them hanging in her eyes.

Her reflection was wearing a golden crown, with an ermine cloak loosely fastened over her, hiding her street clothes.

In her right hand was a scepter.

The rest of them, Daryl, Tracey and Flip sauntered over to where she stood.

"Funny," Flip said, staring into the mirror," I don't see you at all! Just me . . . which is weird because here I am standing right beside you!"

"But I like it! I'm wearing a professional baseball uniform, the Tigers I think! WOW!"

Tracey didn't answer. He was too busy staring at his own reflection which showed him dressed in an airline pilot's uniform. One that was a bit too big.

He smiled broadly and the handsome replica of himself smiled back, waving. He had never to his knowledge told anyone but Daryl that he wanted to fly someday. He'd only been on an airplane once, when his dad had still been alive and they'd flown to Pasadena to visit his grandparents. He'd only been 5, and Eva had been so small she didn't remember flying.

But he did. Since that time he'd read everything he could get his hands on about flying a plane, familiarized himself with all the significant air disasters of the past 20 years and spent his pocket change on the simulated 'flying' games at the local arcade.

Daryl nudged his friend, but Tracey continued to stare into the funhouse mirror, along with Eva and Flip. He couldn't understand what they found so interesting.

When he looked into it over Eva's head he saw nothing. No reflection of any of them, just the rest of the mirrored room behind where they were standing.

"Come ON you guys," he said finally, frustrated. "We just got started! Let's keep going!"

All of them came right away, except for Flip. She seemed to be staring at something in the mirror.

FLIP!" Daryl yelled impatiently, "What are you doing?"

She seemed to jerk to attention, letting out a long breath.

"What the hell?" Daryl said crossly. "What were you staring at?"

For once she didn't seem to have a snappy comeback.

"Nothing….I just thought I saw someone…" she said, smoothing her hair and turning.

The passageway to the rest of the Fun House was located to the left of the mirror they'd been staring into. Tracey took the lead with Daryl staying at his heels. Flip was behind with Eva at her side.

Although it started out narrow, the passage seemed to open up as they continued to walk. It was dim, like a darkroom, the only lighting cast by dull ceramic red light bulbs that caused them all to take on the appearance of being covered in blood.

Tracey thought it was cool, and kept turning around and making scary phantoms of the opera faces at the two girls.

"You're not scaring us, you dork," Flip told him, in her usual superior tone, giving him a shove for emphasis after the second time.

Something dropped down from the ceiling, in front of them, startling them all. In the gloom it took a moment to recognize it. It was moving on spiny segmented legs and had a bulbous body in the center covered with something that seemed like fur.

Its eyes were red.

"AAAAAAAAH!" both Tracey and Daryl yelled at the same time, running forward. The girls stampeded behind them, their hair mere inches from the giant spider's grasp.

When they'd gotten far enough ahead to dare to look behind them, it had disappeared. Or maybe it returned to the cave-like recesses above them that were cloaked in shadow, making it impossible to see what was actually up there.

Flip and Eva were doubled over laughing at their brothers.

"Hahaha, Tracey," Eva laughed. "You scream like a girl! Too funny! Both of you!"

"I wasn't on guard," Tracey explained in his usual affable manner. "Caught me by surprise! Why don't you girls go first so we can have a laugh at you?"

"No problem," Flip said, stepping adroitly past them with Eva," It's a FUN HOUSE guys . . . you have to expect things to jump out at you!"

No sooner had they started walking again than a clown with a hatchet in his hand appeared in front of them. Both the girls shrieked and Eva covered her eyes with her hands.

The clown actually took a swipe at Flip, then disappeared as suddenly as it had appeared.

No sooner had they started walking again than a clown with a hatchet in his hand appeared in front of them. Both the girls shrieked and Eva covered her eyes with her hands. The clown actually took a swipe at Flip, then disappeared as suddenly as it had appeared.

Music came on, some Phantom of the Opera type music, which wound on and on interminably until Flip started getting creeped out. To her logical mind, it didn't make any sense that the attraction wasn't over by now. Hadn't a good twenty minutes gone by?

There was another fork in their path. Everyone stood still for a moment. On the wall, at the point where the path split, there was an ersatz lighted sconce with a portrait of an ugly clown version of the Mona Lisa. She looked like a zombie, scalped on one side, with glowing red eyes. As they stood there arguing about whether to go right or left, two things happened almost at once.

The seemingly two-dimensional portrait of the Clown Mona Lisa moved, first shuddering, then the head pulled up off the background and stood out in relief, the face turning as it smiled at the children, revealing rows of sharpened teeth. While they were still frozen in horror, they heard a roar. Something huge and fur-covered lumbered toward them from the dim entrance of the right-hand passage.

Their screams echoed behind them as they raced to the left.

They kept running past the macabre portraits on the wall, the colorful sconces, and the caged pan character set into an alcove that looked after them imploringly with its yellow eyes as it played on its channel flute. They didn't stop running for five minutes.

When they did, it was because they found themselves at a dead end.

Tracey searched the cavern walls for another passage. In front of them was a good sized red velvet curtain, cordoned off by the same kind of tasseled ropes one might find at an exhibit.

"I think we're screwed, "Tracey said. "We'll have to go back to the other passage, gang. I think it's getting late, too."

Daryl looked at his Timex and frowned, shook it, and frowned again when the hands remained in the same position. It had stopped. He held it to his ear but failed to hear the familiar ticking sound.

"Dammit," he muttered.

He was about to agree with Tracey when some loud organ music cued up, making the girls jump. The curtain parted.

A pleasant-looking man in a ringmaster's uniform strode into the center of the small stage, directly under the spotlight.

"Greetings!" he said, enthusiastically. "It's show time, folks! Thanks for joining us. Welcome to the Dream Weavers Cavalcade of Visions! Sure to impress—and to leave an impression on you for the rest of your lives. Have a SEEEEAT," the ringmaster nearly shouted, gesturing to a half circle of cheap-looking fold-out chairs gathering just outside the circle he was standing in, as if they were expected.

Eva shivered and reached for Flip's hand. There was something about the man that frightened her, even though he was pleasant looking. His voice near the end of his speech had gotten deep and distorted, like a tape that had been slowed down. It made her wonder if he was real or some kind of animatronic, Disney-like thing.

Flip barely felt Eva's hand slipping into hers. She'd been struck mute as soon as the handsome man on the stage had begun speaking. She'd been distracted by the man's appearance. He looked familiar. She noticed that his voice dropped lower at the end of his second short speech, distorting as if he were a life-sized windup toy that was winding down.

The music, seemingly piped in above their heads, suddenly changed to Bach's Tocata and Fugue in D Minor. Daryl gasped as a cylindrical glass tank rose up though the sawdust in the center. Even though the water was greenish and kind of murky he could see fronds of tall underwater plants floating within it, and he could make out something humanoid floating within it also.

It had its back to them, but the short blonde hair floated above its head, waving gently with the motion of the water surrounding it.

Beside him, Tracey threw back his head and laughed delightedly, the two girls joining in as well. A look of confusion crossed Daryl's face. He didn't get what was so amusing about a guy underwater, his bloated looking hands rising and falling as the body twisting around by degrees until he could finally see its equally bloated face.

If Daryl had had anything left in his stomach to regurgitate he would have lost it then. As it was, he sat in his seat, frozen there, too terrified to scream.

The bloated corpse was his cousin, Tom, the one that had drown two summers before up at Kennypaw Lake. It had been a family reunion, and all the kids were swimming, including Eva. The aunts and uncles were scattered around near the shore, under the trees, drinking beers and relaxing in the stout Adirondack chairs as they talked.

Eva had gone in for lemonade, but he was having a great time playing Marco Polo with Tom and his older cousins. When it was his turn to be 'it', he dutifully squinted his eyes closed against the glare the sun was making on the lake, and began calling out.

"MARCO!" he shouted, and for a time he thrashed through the water toward the voices that answered, "POLO," eagerly trying to catch up with one of them.

But time passed and the voices seemed to grow further and further away and then stop altogether. At the same time he noticed that he had gone into the deeper part of the lake and his feet were barely able to touch bottom. It was then he felt something clammy press up against him.

When his eyes flew open he was disoriented at first, amazed to discover how far he'd drifted from the shore. The neatly arranged Adirondack chairs, painted red and blue, still held some of his relatives. And then he'd felt it again, and turned his head. His cousin Tom was floating face up, staring up at him blankly as lake water flowed over not only his face. He didn't try to blink it away or gasp for air. Only his prominent stomach rose above the water.

It was then he realized why Tom wasn't trying to breath. Daryl had started screaming, at the top of his lungs. At first it seemed as if no one could hear him, then one of his uncles jumped to his feet and Daryl could hear him shout to the others.

It had been too late to save Tom, even though two of the uncles were EMTs they couldn't get the water out in time, and so many of the relatives were forced to gather again a few days later for his cousin's funeral.

Daryl found he couldn't tear his eyes away from the figure in front of him, and he could hear the rest of the group, Eva, Flip and Tracey, laughing and hooting. At that moment his cousin, still suspended in the tank, opened his eyes.

Something inside of Daryl snapped. He jumped up, twisting around to grab the metal folding chair he'd been sitting on. Raising it over his head, he ran toward the glass cylinder holding his cousin, and smashed it into the tank, turning his face away so that he wouldn't be hit by any shards.

There was silence for a moment, even the piped in music stopped, and when Daryl opened them again his visual field was completely filled with Flip's angry face.

"DARYL! YOU ASSHOLE!" she raged," What the hell are you doing, trying to kill that little dog?"

Daryl blinked. In the ring he saw a tiny poodle wearing a clown costume cowering behind a disapproving ringmaster. The ringmaster was making soothing sounds to calm the puppy and glaring malevolently at Daryl.

Tracey and Eva were doing the same.

He put the chair down, stuttering, "S-S-S-S-SEE it? D-d-didn't you s-s-s-ee?" he asked, his voice shaking.

"Have you gone queer?" Tracey demanded. "Who attacks a circus puppy with a chair? What did it ever do to you?"

The ringmaster chose that moment to point toward the exit.

"Show's over folks," he said matter-of-factly.

As the group departed through the curtain, Flip gave Daryl a swift kick in the shin.

"Thanks, Daryl," she said disgustedly. "Best part of the attraction and you had to lose your mind!"

"Yeah-WTF dude?" Tracey said, flanking him. "Show's over now! Thanks a lot!"

"I saw . . . I saw something," Daryl said. "I didn't see a dog, I'm telling you! I saw my cousin Tom—the one that drowned two summers ago…I swear I saw him! I swear to God!"

All three of the others stopped, making a half circle around him and staring at him.

"You've gone mental then," Tracey finally said, snorting. "No more fun houses for YOU!"

The group walked back toward the fork in the passage, expecting to take the turn out of the funhouse, but instead they found themselves in a hall with a long mirror along one side, and three doors.

"What the hell?" Tracey exclaimed.

Eva looked up at Phillipa, who was staring intently at what seemed to be her own reflection in the long mirror.

"Yes, I understand," she was saying, as the others looked on, perplexed. "But I don't care! Nothing has been the same since you left! Nothing! And mother is intolerable!"

As the group watched Flip's reflection in the mirror, a man appeared behind her reflection. Placing his hands on her shoulders from behind.

Daryl ran up beside his sister, his eyes wide with incredulity as he gazed at the reflection.

"DAD!' he blurted.

He was still staring at the image of his father. His father smiling back at him and winked.

"I'll take good care of her," he said. "You need to stay Daryl. Your mother will need you. But I want my girl with me."

At what precise moment, Flip vanished at his side and all that remained of her was her own reflection *in the mirror*. Daryl wouldn't be able to recall afterwards, but one moment she'd been there, and the next she had somehow joined her mirrored reflection, hugging her father, then slipping her hand into his as they turned to go, a look of sublime happiness on her face.

Eva and Tracey were silent as the trio watched Phillipa, her hand in her father's, walk further and further away into an unseen terrain.

When they were far enough away that they seemed very small, Daryl saw his father turn around to look behind him one last time. But it wasn't his father's face Daryl saw. It was the face of the clown that had frightened the girls earlier. He was leering, a macabre impression of a smile, exposing rows of jagged pointy teeth and nodding in satisfaction.

"No!" Daryl, Tracey and Eva screamed together, pounding on the glass.

"FLIP COME BACK!' Eva wailed, scratching at the glass, "That's not your DAD!"

Tracey pushed off the glass and turned to Daryl. For the first time he looked frightened.

"Look," he said tersely, "There is something really wrong with this place. It's playing with our heads. I hope this is a hoax and Flip is somewhere else, but for now we need to get OUT of here, you hear me?"

"Agreed," Daryl said. Although he was stunned that Flip seemed to have disappeared, he thought she would turn up and he was glad that Tracey had seen what he had seen because that meant he might believe that Daryl had seen his cousin.

They turned and realized that instead of an open passage they were facing three identical doors.

"What's behind door number one, I wonder," Tracey said, in a low voice, as if he were speaking to himself.

He pulled on the handle. The door opened, and there was Mrs. Prescott.

"Oh, there you are!" she said. "I thought I would have to come in after you all! Tracey and Eva go ahead and get in the car! I want to have a word with Daryl please!"

Looking relieved, Tracey took Eva's hand and moved past his mother. Behind Mrs. Prescott's shoulder Daryl could see daylight, people moving past the Funhouse attraction, and the parking lot.

Just seeing the sky outside made him feel calmer.

"Now then, Mr. Daryl," she said, closing the door behind her and leaning on it. "I have a bone to pick with you, mister!"

Daryl found himself sweating.

"Sorry?" he said. She didn't look mad, he thought. He was thinking that it was strange that she hadn't noticed that Flip wasn't with them when she spoke again.

"I've seen the way you look at me, Daryl," she said, moving toward him, her voice becoming silky smooth. "I think that you have been thinking dirty little thoughts about me. Am I right?"

Daryl couldn't speak. She was right of course, but it was one thing to think about his best friend's mother when he was alone in his bed at night, and quite another to have her call him out on it in person.

He dropped his head.

"I don't know what to say," he answered.

She began walking around him, circling him.

"You're tall for your age," she said. "And I think someday soon that baby fat is going to fall off and you will be quite the stud. Tell me, when you think about me naked, what do my tits look like? Do they look anything like this?"

Daryl's head jerked up without his willing it to, and he watched as Mrs. Prescott unbuttoned her blouse and pulled her bra up, revealing a splendid pair of tip tilted breasts with pink nipples. She reached forward, capturing his instant erection in her hand and giving it a painful squeeze.

"Take it out, Daryl," she told him. "I want to see how you're growing."

Without knowing how he'd gotten there, Daryl found himself lying on the floor, his pants and underwear pulled down to his kneecaps while Tracey and Eva's mother straddled him. He groaned as he felt for the first time her wet velvet interior.

For most of the incredible experience his eyes were closed. The sensations were overwhelming. He moaned as he erupted, but she didn't stop riding him and he quickly became excited again.

He was on the verge of his second orgasm when he finally opened his eyes and looked up so he could see her boobs again.

Daryl screamed.

The woman on top of him was not Mrs. Prescott. In fact it wasn't a woman at all. It was the Mona Lisa clown that had come to life and attacked them from her place on the wall.

He shriveled up, his prick so terrified it felt as though it were trying to retract as far back into his body as possible. She was gone, instantly. He jerked the door open and ran for daylight, his pants still around his knees.

***

Phillippa was never found, despite a thorough search by law enforcement authorities and an injunction shutting the entire carnival down.

Eva started speaking again after six months and intensive sessions with a Childhood Trauma Expert and Speech Therapist.

Tracey developed cataracts after having a detached retina repaired and lost 68% of his vision in his right eye. He put his dreams of becoming a pilot on hold.

Daryl doesn't sleep well at night. Nothing that his doctor prescribes seems to work. His drowned cousin Tom has taken up permanent residence in one corner of his room, and throughout the night no headphones or earbuds or other devices can drown out the sound of the lake water dripping off his dead cousin's bloated body and onto the carpet. All night long, all he hears is, drip . . . drip . . . drip.

53

The Night

Ric Wasley

The Night
Ric Wasley

Author's Note

The clock has just struck twelve, and it is now officially Halloween.

And now that midnight has ticked by, I find myself in a darkly romantic mood. Not really the physical side of romance, but the intense psychic side. The kind that fills dark dreams of souls possessed by passions that can consume you from the inside out.

Passions articulated by Byron, Keats and, of course, Percy Bysshe Shelly and his lovely nineteen-year-old bride, Mary.

One night during the summer of 1816, in the midst of a torential rain that split the heavens, a group of young poets and writers sat before a dwindling fire in an old manse overlooking Lake Geneva. Deep in the grip of a fey spirit or insurmountable ennui, they dared one another to craft the most dire, chilling tale imaginable. While it is not recorded precisely what the terms of the wager or the fate of the losing stories were, there is no doubt today whose tale has succeeded in spanning the years to resonate so resoundingly in each and every tale of terror that haunts our nightmares but thrills our imagination.

Mary Shelly called her story *The Modern Prometheus*. We know it by its more popular name: *Frankenstein*.

So, in homage to Mary's spirit as well as the other early greats such as Edgar Allen Poe and Bram Stoker, who gave us tales to chill our blood and send our hearts racing, I offer up the following.

****

Dark claws of tree branches rattle at every window. Demon-driven wind lashes the roof and drives the smoke from the slumbering fire back down the chimney, where it hangs about the overhead beams and collects in the corners of the room. The smoke sends sinuous black tendrils to curl about my head and tickle the corners of my eyes. It makes me think of . . . her.

I see her once more standing before the fireplace, just as she appeared the last night that she walked the earth. Her skin so white it shone like alabaster in the flickering firelight. Her long dark hair curling to her waist in raven black tresses. Eyes, an ice-water blue, and bone-white teeth showing between her parted, blood-red lips.

* * * *

Her eyes stared back at mine with a gaze that was not so much an accusation as sadness. We have both hurt one another terribly, though her stare was a reaction to consuming loneliness, while mine ?

She waited for me to speak, to give a reason. But lust knows no reason, no rhyme, only the small gnawing animal that consumes you, bite by tiny inexorable bite.

She had asked me why I had forsaken the vow I'd sworn not twelve months ago. How could I explain? How could I answer? What reason could I give?

"Am I not pleasing in your eyes?"

"God knows you are all that and more," I answered.

"Is my grace and form not that of someone you could love?"

I could only shake my head.

"Did I not come to your bed each night you wanted me with love, devotion, and passion?"

I nodded.

She stretched out both arms, the sheer black lace shimmering from each arm giving her the appearance of a crucified dark angel. "Why?"

Why, why, why?

"You!" I blurted out. "Your obsession with darkness and all things of the night!" I peered at her porcelain skin—smooth, unblemished, and . . . white. A dead, bloodless white. The only thing of color in her face, those beautiful blood-red lips. How many nights had I spent kissing those perfect lips? Lips that seemed to grow redder and redder with each deepening kiss. But when the morning sun trickled through the window, the pillow beside me was always empty. And when I knocked at the locked door of the shuttered room down the hall, I never gained any answer.

I looked up. Her ice-blue eyes continued to stare in sad resignation. "If you found no pleasure in my embrace you had only to tell me. I would sooner release you than force you into the arms of another." She bowed her head. "What is it that a yellow-haired farmer's daughter can give you that you feel I cannot?"

"Life!" I said. "Life—and laughter! An open face and a smile that lights up in the sunshine. The sunshine that you shun like a pestilence. You lie secluded in your dark and shuttered room all day and only grace me with your company at dinner."

"But do I not provide lively companionship and stimulating conversation over dinner? And you yourself have complimented me on my skill on the piano forte."

"Lively," I murmured.

Her gaze sharpened for an instant then quickly softened as she whispered, "And did I not bring you nights of sweetness beyond measure?"

How could I deny it? I had become besotted with her charms and begun to live only for the night until I could stand it no longer.

And that was why I had to break free. Free from her. Free from the night and free from my own doubts that turned a dagger of suspicion through my entrails until the only way I could solace them was to find revenge and release in the arms of a simple sun-dappled farm girl who kissed me in green fields under blue sunlit skies.

"I can forgive everything, but why did you have to wound me with deception?"

"Deception?" I exploded. "You dare speak to me of deception? You who locks me out of your room each day while you do God knows what with God knows who. You—"

"Is that what you think?" she asked softly, shaking her head.

"What else can I think?" I snarled.

Her eyes grew sadder, and she sighed in resignation, though her chest neither rose nor fell. There was the faint smell of flowers just before they close their petals at dusk. Her scent.

"Very well," she said. "Meet me tomorrow, and I will prove my love—and my fidelity."

"Where?"

"I will wait for you by the stone bench that sits beside the old graveyard at the top of the hill."

I think that she knew what my next words would be before I even spoke them. "When?"

She smiled sadly. "Whenever you wish."

How often I have wished that I could have called my next words back. "Noon. When the sun is highest overhead."

She slowly nodded. "If that is what it takes to prove my love, then so be it."

She did not come to me that night, and when I awoke the sun was already well-risen and the morning hour late.

I dressed hastily, hurried downstairs, and pulled open the front door just as the hall clock struck noon. I rushed down the garden path and up the well-worn track that led to the graveyard hill and my one true love.

My one true love…

Suddenly my heart constricted with nameless dread. What had I done? Perhaps she had some strange malady of the skin that might blister and mar in sunlight. Or some internal disease of the heart or liver which required rest and darkness. Or….

I reached the crest of the hill. The old graveyard covered most of the hilltop. The gray stone fence, tumbled and askew in some places, surrounded the eastern side, and next to a tall weathered monument near the crest sat an ornately carved stone bench.

But it was empty.

My heart pounded wildly. She had grown tired of waiting and left….but no, the faint chimes of the church steeple clock tolled the last stroke of noon, the sound drifting up from the village below.

I shaded my eyes with my hand and searched for some sign of life or movement. I thought bitterly: *Life. Mine is as empty and devoid of life as the dead stones beside me.* She had become sickened by my infidelity and left me. Or perhaps had met her own lover at this spot and decided to seek happiness and love elsewhere.

I buried my head in my hands and sank down onto the bench. The cold stone chilled me, but the sun hung bright and made each feature of the hill stand out in sharp relief. And that was when I noticed it. Her shawl. Deep wine red, made of Spanish lace, and it had been my gift to her on our wedding day. If she had run off, why had she left it here? Then I saw the other things . . . one of her tiny black slippers stuck in a crevice in the stone wall. I walked over and picked it up. But it was what I saw on the other side of the wall that struck me like a pistol ball through the heart. Her best black silk dress spread out just inside the old graveyard lying peacefully as if the owner had lain down to take a pleasant nap in the sun.

An empty dress.

My mind reeled. How? Why? Where could she have gone, naked to the sun and sky and ….? I realized then that the dress was not empty.

I knelt down and scooped up a pale powder from the neckline of the dress. I rubbed it between my fingers. Ash.

At the end of one lacy sleeve I spotted a glint of gold. I sifted the object from the ash.

Her wedding ring.

* * * *

The storm is passing now. The branches have ceased their tapping at my window, but still I sit—and wait. I am waiting for another tap that I know some night will come. It must come!

I seldom venture forth during the daylight hours. What is the point? She will not be there, waiting for me in the sunlight.

But at night, that is where she will be waiting, in the cool, soft velvet darkness of the night.

And so I close my eyes and wait for a butterfly caress upon my cheek . . . and when I open my eyes, she will be standing there, and we will be together—forever.

In the night.

Mr. Rumples

George Larson

Mr. Rumples

George Larson

I couldn't see Mr. Rumples' countenance given the many layers of greasepaint on his face. His face bore bumps and protrusions that defied explanation. They stuck out at different places and angles to exhibit a certain, off-putting grotesquerie, at least for me. His nose was abbreviated and his dark eyes were deeply sunk into the sockets. The red greasepaint or rouge around them gave him a macabre look. They were the focal point for his face and I winced when I looked into them from time to time. Maybe he had a serious skin condition that he was trying to hide from his young audience so as not to scare them. Or maybe they were simply small prosthetics he had applied beforehand. I didn't know, but I was intrigued by the ersatz costume that he invariably wore during each of his performances for the children of Westlake, Pennsylvania.

It wasn't a traditional one for a run-of-the-mill clown by any stretch of the imagination. It consisted of a rumpled, oversized, gray sports coat with baggy gray trousers. Maybe it suited his name too, just part of his shtick. In any case, it looked like he bought it at a secondhand clothing store during a fire sale. The jacket sleeves were so long they covered his hands. His dwarf-like body with a shaggy, orange wig atop his head simply added more of a mystique to this entertainer of the young. The kids seemed to be enthralled and absolutely mesmerized by him and his getup, but the parents less so. He wore tooth overlays that made it appear he had filed his front teeth into forms of sharp V's which added to his freakish persona. I thought he was a bit creepy, but the kids absolutely loved him.

Well, so much for taste these days. It must be a generational thing. Maybe kids brought up on a constant diet of monsters, superheroes, creatures of all stripes, alien beings, and the like, didn't find Mr. Rumples to be a strange figure in the slightest. I couldn't figure it out.

I never much cared for clowns when I was young. There was something about them that elicited fear rather than excitement and joy in me. I don't know what it was about them that frightened me, but that nagging feeling still resided way down deep inside of me. So why was I watching this clown's performance today if I disliked clowns so much? The short answer is that I had to since it was part of my investigation into bizarre events happening in my community; body snatchings to be precise.

My name's Harry Balt and I am a grade III detective on the Westlake Police Department. I was standing in the backyard of Susie Miller's house at her 8th birthday party and Mr. Rumples was the star attraction. I blended in well with the parents who were watching their kids while waiting for Mr. Rumples' grand entrance. This would be my second attendance at one of his shows. I hoped it would be the last and I could write him off as a subject of interest. I simply hated freaking clowns! Perhaps my loathing of them was a full-blown phobia, but a label wasn't necessary to describe my visceral dislike of his ilk.

All of a sudden, it was show time and the clown rushed from the house. "I'm Mr. Rumples, a magician extraordinaire. Watch closely for my tricks and don't have a care. I'm all kiddies pal, best friend of the young. Come to my magical world and enjoy the fun!" He repeated the ditty a few times while prancing around the children who sat on the grass at his feet. He next tossed whirligigs and gimcracks to the kids, who delighted in snatching up as many of the tchotchkes as they could hold in their small hands. They'd enjoy the swag later when they got home.

However, I couldn't help but notice the spittle coming from his mouth as he spoke the words. It ran down the lower portion of his face causing streaks in the greasepaint. That resulted in even more melodrama to his face, if that were possible. The kids didn't seem to notice or didn't mind. It was all about Mr. Rumples, their center of attraction and their world at the moment, and nothing more. As Mr. Rumples chanted and circled the children, he abruptly stopped directly in front of the birthday girl and curtsied in a theatrical manner. As he did so, he brought out a candied egg from under his jacket and presented the gift to Susie Miller. She beamed and readily accepted the present and politely thanked Mr. Rumples for his kindness. Mr. Rumples then kissed her lightly on the cheek before once more continuing his routine. Susie Miller would fondly remember Mr. Rumples for the rest of her short life.

Mr. Rumples' act proceeded without interruption for the next hour or so to the amusement of the crowd. The parents politely clapped at his juggling of balls, spinning of pie plates, the rabbit in the hat trick and all the other routine, hokey tricks that would never make Mr. Rumples a star on the Vegas Strip. He'd occasionally pull a golden flute from his jacket pocket and play a little tune that I didn't recognize. I found it to be a bit eerie and noticed the children's eyes following the seductive movement of the flute as it moved back and forth in front of them. He was like a snake charmer or the Pied Piper of Hamlin. The flute had a hypnotic effect on the youngsters that couldn't be denied, at least as far as I was concerned. But the children were delighted with his performance. Mr. Rumples could do no wrong in their eyes. He was a local hero and superstar and perhaps much more than met their young eyes.

I was struck by one thing while observing Mr. Rumples in action. Actually, it was something that was missing—his hands. His jacket sleeves drooped at least a foot below where his hands should have been. He occasionally flapped his sleeves at the end of a trick and the audience ate up his foolishness with glee. But I never once saw his hands, even while he juggled the balls and spun the plates. I guessed he had somehow mastered such things, but I couldn't figure out how he did it without exposing his hands. Maybe he had deformities that he didn't want to reveal to the children. I simply didn't know, but the fact intrigued me.

***

It was early Fall in Westlake with a beautiful Indian summer in progress. The trees still held most of their leaves and no one cared at the moment if winter was fast approaching. Fall was a fun time and Halloween a big event for most of the townspeople who fully participated in its pageantry. Homes were decked out in witches, goblins, ghosts, a mummy or two and, of course, the ubiquitous jack-o-lanterns. Even the town center was festooned with bundles of cornstalks, gourds, pumpkins and spider webs, along with spooky music playing from loudspeakers in the park. Fortunately, the ACLU hadn't found any civil rights violations in our bucolic community so we continued celebrating Halloween each year without fear of being slapped with a lawsuit.

But I wasn't in the mood for such festivities this year since I was getting almost nowhere on my investigation. Westlake was not a cesspool of serious crime to put things into quick perspective. During my 10 years on the force, the most serious crimes were domestic violence, suicides and a handful of B&Es. Major crimes happened in Pittsburgh, some 20 miles east of our little town. But things had changed over the past few months and now the town was faced with a puzzling mystery--horrific crimes perpetrated in our own backyard, so to speak. They were inexplicable and I was the designated detective to sort them out. Well, technically speaking, I was the only detective on the force. Now I was stuck with a messy, tar baby of a case. Sometimes life plays cruel tricks on those who protect and serve.

The first case of a missing body from the Westlake Community Cemetery was reported about three months ago. The cemetery was a municipal, nondenominational one that has been in operation for over 100 years. While on the face of it, a missing body might be explained by an error in recordkeeping in the plot assignments or possibly an authorized move of a body to another cemetery at a relative's request. But those explanations didn't wash in this instance. Lucy Ambrose's body was missing! I spent much time examining the records and interviewing the cemetery staff at length. Lucy's corpse had disappeared into thin air or so it seemed and no one had a clue as to its whereabouts. Lucy was 9 years old at the time of her death. She had succumbed to a severe case of pneumonia and died after a short bout with the disease. The virus that struck her down resisted the latest antibiotics and that greatly worried the medical authorities.

A cemetery maintenance worker discovered that the topsoil of her gravesite had been disturbed, maybe more than just disturbed. The worker thought that a large animal, perhaps a bear, had dug into the grave given the large piles of dirt surrounding it. Bear had been sighted in the general vicinity, but they were still fairly shy and only raided the local garbage dump on the edge of town. He also observed marks in the well-manicured grass that a rake might make or maybe the claws of a large bear.

So who or what could have caused such damage in a relatively short period of time? It was decided to exhume Lucy's body to determine how deep the animal had dug into the grave and if her casket and remains had been disturbed. I was present at the exhumation and I was totally freaked out when the backhoe delivered her casket above ground and unceremoniously plopped it at our feet. There was no Lucy inside, only what appeared to be her funerary garments and nothing else! Even her pair of black Mary Janes was present and accounted for. The clothing was entirely intact and no ripping or tearing was evident. The bear (or whatever or whoever it was) had undressed Lucy and dragged her naked body out of the ground. It had obviously tunneled into the grave and out again with Lucy's body in tow. Good God, how could that be?

I wasn't ready to suspend my credulity, at least then. There had to be a logical answer to this mystery. I didn't have a clue as to what that might be, but I'd give my best shot to unravel this conundrum. This case was way beyond my experience and pay grade and I needed help—soonest. I immediately contacted the Allegheny County Sheriff's Office and requested their forensic team's assistance. They showed up at the scene rather quickly and I suspected they were intrigued by my phone call. And they certainly should have been. I had already strung the perfunctory, yellow tape around the gravesite and sternly warned the workers not to breach its perimeter and not to let anyone else do so on pain of receiving many parking tickets and/or moving violations.

They seemed to take my hollow threat seriously and that was good. Contamination of a crime scene was the number one bugaboo for the forensic technicians. I then went to the department's database to determine how many instances of grave desecrations had been reported over the past 5 years. Surprisingly, there were only a few and these were typically committed by teenagers out on a summer drunk. These were misdemeanor offenses with the perpetrators usually let off with a warning, a slap on the wrist, along with paying for any damage they caused to headstones or other objects in the cemetery. I'd check these out, but suspected I wouldn't find anything useful.

George Heron telephoned me the next day to report the first, small bit of forensic results. It may have been small, but it was a significant finding. George headed the Allegheny County Forensics Lab and we had known each other for a few years. He was one of the good guys in the biz and we got along well and trusted each other. He was 90% Allegheny Indian and he and his family had lived in the area for generations. How he determined he was 90% Allegheny was unknown to me. But I accepted his claim at face value. George quipped about his lineage by saying a white man must have gotten into one of his ancestor's loincloth many generations ago and that accounted for the miscegenation. Despite his corny joke, I respected and liked him very much. I hoped the sentiments were mutual.

"You really have a real pisser on your hands, Harry," he spoke with unaccented English in a politically incorrect manner. That's another thing I liked about him.

"We found two hairs in the casket that were inconsistent with Lucy. By the way, the test concluded the hairs were not human, maybe animal, maybe synthetic, but most certainly not human in origin. We're putting the samples through additional testing to determine their origin, but don't hold your breath because it will take us a couple of weeks to nail them down. We're also running down some latent prints found on and inside the casket and that's going to take us awhile too because of the process of elimination. Be patient Harry, but be assured you'll get every bit of evidence we can tease from the scene. I thought you might want this first piece of info sooner than later."

Of course, he was spot on, as usual. George and I chitchatted for a few more minutes about nothing in particular. That was fine with me since I couldn't make heads or tails of what he just told me. Maybe it was a bear after all. If the hairs weren't human, they had to be animal or synthetic in origin. *OK, right, but what kind of animal or wig*, I wondered.

***

Dr. Allen Gensch wasn't particularly liked or respected in Westlake. Truthfully, most people hated his freaking guts. His residing in Pittsburg and commuting to our fair town bolstered that fact. He was the medical director of The Cummings Clinic, a family planning and abortion mill located close to the center of town. The police were thoroughly familiar with the clinic given the number of threats against the doctor's life and the many angry protests outside the clinic's doors.

Dr. Gensch called the department's switchboard early Monday morning and frantically related to the 911 operator that the clinic had been robbed over the weekend. The operator emotionally flinched when he told her 4 aborted fetuses had been stolen from the clinic's walk-in freezer. Of course, I caught the call as usual and responded to the scene of the crime. It was only a 2 minute drive from my office so I made the trip in record time without lights and siren, although I'd liked to have used them just for the hell of it. Maybe someday I'd get my chance.

A hand-printed "Temporarily Closed" sign was taped to the clinic's front entrance. Someone had already marked through the word "Temporarily." The sentiments of the townspeople had come to the fore again. Dr. Gensch greeted me at the front door with an unsmiling face. "So what are you going to do about this outrageous act, detective? The antiabortionists have gone too far and are now criminals in the eyes of the law. There's money on the table here and I want those fetuses returned immediately. I have outstanding orders for them. I also want the perpetrators arrested and tried for their crimes. I operate a legal business and I pay more than my fair share of taxes to Westlake."

I didn't directly respond to his ranting and merely told him that a full and thorough investigation would be conducted with the aim of identifying and apprehending those responsible for the crime. It was a stock answer and nothing more. I didn't think he deserved more. The doctor escorted me to the rear of the building and it was quickly evident how the robber or robbers had entered the premises. The large metal clad door that lay in the alleyway was bent, battered and scratched up. The doctor told me that the clinic took security matters very seriously, especially because of the protests by the antiabortionists.

Actually he said, "Those fucking antiabortionist, fanatical bastards," but I paraphrased his statement for the sake of brevity in my report. The doctor went on to say that the door in question had been reinforced with two long-throw sliding deadbolts and the exterior hinge pins had been spot-welded to prevent removal of them along with the door itself. I asked if there was CCTV camera coverage on the building's exterior perimeter and he replied no. Well so much for high security measures. However, the doctor stated that the clinic had installed a state-of-the-art intrusion detection alarm some three months ago, although he allowed it was only a local alarm because he considered the monthly monitoring fees to be onerous and a waste of money. He then repeated his vitriolic language in case I'd missed his initial venting. I got it loud and clear the first time around. I didn't bother to suggest that if the alarm had sounded, his neighbors likely wouldn't have responded.

I examined the door (or what remained of it), the door jambs, the hinges along with the scattered debris. It was obvious that the door had been pulled outward from its frame. Given the gouge marks and scratches on the leading door edge and one jamb, the perps may have used pry bars to gain entry. However, I believed a combination of devices removed the door. A chain hooked onto a pickup truck and the door was one explanation, but I didn't see any tire tracks indicating such. Still, a combination of pry bars and a pull chain might be the answer. Perhaps a carjack spanning the vertical jambs and spreading them open was also a possibility. In any case, more than one bad guy was involved in the break-in, unless Superman had moved to the dark side of the law.

It was now time to see the location of the thefts and I wasn't looking forward to it one bit. I dutifully walked three paces behind Dr. Gensch and we soon reached the cooler. He opened the door and invited me inside. I immediately saw clear plastic bags stacked on shelves containing the tiny bodies of aborted fetuses. My stomach did a couple of quick barrel rolls before I regained my composure and breakfast. I noticed the doctor watching me and caught a smarmy smirk on his face. He seemed to be amused at my distress. I was surprised since if my face had turned a bilious green, I was convinced it was Daddy Warbucks favorite color. So go figure.

"I lost 4 units that were ready for shipment this week," the doctor explained without any prompting. *Oh my God, units? Is that what it came down to in the doctor's calculating mind? It seemed production numbers and delivery schedules ruled his world,* I thought. But I kept my mouth shut despite his cold reference to the unborn laying in the freezer. "Oddly, all were female," he added.

"Why just four fetuses when there are many more here? Why steal only female fetuses?"

"I have no clue. You're the detective so you tell me," he snottily replied. I clenched my fists and held them tightly at my sides fearing I might lose my temper and control at the same time. I had ten years invested on the force and didn't want to be sacked for committing a youthful indiscretion. At my age, I was much too old to qualify for one. Moreover, I didn't think my superiors or the court would graciously accept my innocence plea and punch line.

The doctor correctly surmised I didn't like his retort so he changed topics and related a little bit of information about the fetus trade. It was only a business and nothing more, he assured me.

"The clinic is a for-profit business enterprise that offers reasonably priced abortions on demand. Sure, we go through the litany about a woman's choices and options, but frankly most opt for abortions. That's the reality of the situation. The fetus and placenta are the end products that we seek. Our abortion fees cover much of our general operating costs, but the real money is in the end products we sell to research laboratories and medical colleges around the world. Stem cell harvesting is big business these days. We maintain high standards by offering quality service, absolutely unadulterated fetuses and timely delivery of our products to our customers at competitive prices."

I suspected I'd just heard the beginning of his marketing spiel. It sounded like the doctor was blithely describing the business plan and promotion strategies for Oscar Meyer wieners and not fetuses. Then again, maybe the two were similar, at least in his mind. After all, it was simply the purveyance of meat and nothing more.

And I'd heard enough.

I stepped out of the freezer and placed a call to George Heron, once again requesting assistance from his forensic team. I briefed him on my findings. He said his dance card was pretty full, but he'd get his people to the crime scene shortly. I thanked him and hung up. I then turned to Dr. Gensch and explained what was about to happen at his clinic--it was now a crime scene and people couldn't enter without my explicit permission. He initially balked at closing the clinic, but he had no choice in the matter and realized it was no use to try to browbeat me into changing my mind.

I carelessly dropped my business card at his feet. And I warned him not to leave town without checking with me first. I admit I like using that throwaway line from time to time. I now had duly done my due diligence diligently. My clever alliteration probably confused him, it certainly did me. I then shook his hand while smiling and he grimaced in pain. I had a very firm grip when I needed one. This guy needed one. Actually, my smile was more of a shit-eating grin. I felt better than I had all morning.

***

This was all too bizarre. Two cases of bodysnatching had occurred in a span of a few weeks. I wasn't sure the cases were related, but my sharp Occam's razor suggested they were in some inexplicable way. I was already getting jabs from my coworkers about alien abductions or the Rapture being responsible for the disappearances. None of them believed a rogue bear was responsible. I still thought it was an implausible theory of the crime as well. But something strange was happening and I was stumped for answers. Luckily, the information regarding the cases was still maintained in-house, but I wasn't sure for how long. Eventually, the media hounds would get a sniff of the story and then all hell would break loose. The cemetery and the clinic had stayed mum and for good reason. New business was at stake for both of them.

I researched reports of bodysnatching in the U.S. and had a few hits, but none resembled my cases. Bodies certainly had monetary value and maybe that's what all of this was about. Unscrupulous buyers and unscrupulous sellers could make serious money in a cadaver transaction. Body parts commanded top dollar by bypassing laws and regulations governing their sale. If caught, the lawbreakers typically received fines or lenient sentences, again, only if they got caught. It appeared there was a thriving underground industry afoot, no puns intended. History, especially in England, had many examples of grave robbers who plied their trade for profit. The internet searches were interesting, but they didn't bring me any closer to solving the mystery. I was frustrated and needed some luck to break my way. And maybe that was about to happen.

Mr. Rumples had popped up on my radar screen as a person of interest. I thought he was a long shot as a candidate for the crimes, but he was someone I was looking into. I was grasping at all of those straws at the moment. There were a couple of other straws I was focusing on as well, but Mr. Rumples was a very intriguing character. Why did he interest me?

There were a couple of things, both very tentative and sketchy at best. As I could tell, he showed up in Westlake a few months ago from parts unknown. He simply appeared in our town of about 3,500 souls. Everyone knew everyone and their business here. Gossip traveled fast in these parts. That's just the way things worked in a small and usually tight knit community. But Mr. Rumples was the odd man out, both literally and figuratively speaking; fundamentally, he was a very quirky, mysterious figure among us. No one knew much about him, but he quickly established a following on the internet with the children of Westlake. That fact intrigued me and piqued my interest. I'd check him out along with other leads and persons of interest.

***

Here was another of those straws that I found interesting. It looked like my best, vague lead at the moment. Maybe my hypothesis was merely wishful thinking. Regardless, I really had no other ideas to gain traction. More than a dozen rail companies transited or stopped at Westlake at its southern border. The hobos and vagabonds who detrained in our town had caused the citizenry worries and concerns for many years. However, their worries far outweighed the actual instances of crime in our community. But we couldn't fully convince them of that fact despite our best PR efforts.

Our town had long served as a railhead for the lines where trains from both the west and east switched tracks to continue their onward journeys. Most of the illegal riders were simply down on their luck and life, looking for nothing more than a fresh chance to rebuild their lives and start anew. But there were a few bad actors among the downtrodden of this world. Yes, there were criminals and former convicts who rode the rails. There were also railroad gangs that controlled and intimidated the other freebooters in the boxcars. And yes, there were many illegal aliens as well. But all-in-all, they didn't present our town with any serious problems.

Fortunately, these bad guys were far and few between according to our police blotter. But convincing the populace otherwise was an overwhelming, impossible task. However, maybe one or more of these transients had been responsible for the horrific crimes. I was now referring to more than one actor in this drama since the break-in at the clinic had to involve more than one person. They certainly had opportunity and mobility to carry out such acts.

To me, the obvious motive was money. They could deliver their ghastly cargo to customers by simply riding the rails throughout the United States. And ironically, there would be no shipping charges involved! Were they clever enough to store the bodies in the train's reefers to preserve them? Yes, a gang might very well be responsible for the crimes, I theorized.

***

I wasn't sleeping so well and my appetite had waned over the past several weeks. Maybe the stress of the case was causing a bout of anxiety and depression. My bosses upstairs were pressuring me to close the case as soon as possible or sooner. In cop-speak that didn't mean solving the case, only bringing it to a conclusion that the big suits could accept and artfully defend with the media. Plausible denial was another tactic the department was very adept at using if necessary. That's how things worked around here. I believed I might be the fall guy riding the scapegoat in this theater of the absurd. That didn't sit well with me.

I continued to pursue the hobo angle and sent out short faxes to the various railroad police departments that served Westlake. I summarized the crimes and asked if they could provide any useful thoughts or leads. I had already notified the Pittsburgh FBI office and regional law enforcement agencies with similar information and requests for assistance. So far those efforts had come to naught.

I Googled railroad hobos and tramps and found some interesting information. There had been much written about the subculture, but I was struck by one item in particular: the way they communicated with each other in signs and symbols. They had a language of their own that could be easily deciphered by their brethren. A symbol of a triangle with stick arms meant there was a man with a gun; a hash mark warned that a police officer lived in the house; a simple T sign indicated that the owner would offer food for work; a large C denoted the home's owner was gone; and three slash marks told others that it was a unsafe area. Of course, there were many more signals that filled in the hobo lexicon. According to my reading, the signs were typically applied with white chalk. A good rain later would erase them and that suited the vagabonds' desire for anonymity. The last thing they wanted was to bring attention to their presence.

If organized gangs of hobos had committed the crimes, it was just possible they had used signs and symbols to communicate with each other. Maybe, just maybe I might find some evidence at the scenes. I started my search at the Westlake Community Cemetery where Lucy Ambrose's body had been dug up. Since her burial was only recent, the grave robbers would have had a much easier time burrowing into the soft ground and removing her small corpse.

It was a hunch, but the only possible lead I had to work with back then. So I visited the cemetery once again to determine if hobo signals were present. I started my search at its epicenter, Lucy's gravesite, and expanded my examination of the grounds, trees and headstones outward at increments of 10 yards. I marked my progress using small utility flags so I didn't have to backtrack and be reasonably assured of the integrity of my search pattern. Regrettably, I was unable to find any evidence of hobo activity.

I did notice that a couple of headstones had been defaced by being tagged with red florescent paint, likely thanks to one or more of our upstanding youth. I next moved on to the clinic and conducted a similar search with similar results. Well, so much for my hunch. But the hobos were still high on my list of suspects and I would run the theory to ground. My cop colleagues teased that I was like a bulldog with lockjaw when it came to pursing an investigation. I think that meant I was one stubborn SOB and they were right.

***

The stinky, brown stuff had just hit the fan and I was in the center of a vortex of one massive shit storm that now swirled around our little town. The weekly Westlake Gazette had just published a story about the bodysnatching phenomena on its front page. The story had some fact, but a lot of speculation about the crimes that didn't help matters one iota. The article was downright lurid in its gory details. So much so, the department's switchboard was lighting up like a fully decorated Christmas tree.

Callers were asking if the story was true and, if so, what were we doing about it. People were anxious and frightened and understandably so. No events of this magnitude had ever happened in Westlake. Given my normal paranoia, I smelled a rat. One of my cop buddies most likely had leaked the story to the Gazette.

Maybe buddy wasn't the correct term; *turd* might be more apropos in this instance. Moreover, Halloween was fast approaching and its putative connection to the story wasn't lost on the ordinary citizen. It seemed the entire town was going bonkers! As for me, my daily diet now consisted of black coffee, Pepto-Bismol and cigarettes, followed by a Xanax or two. To state the obvious, I wasn't doing so well and neither was my investigation.

***

Just as I thought things couldn't get any worse, they went to shit again, but pardon the scatological reference to my particular situation. My world seemed to be painted over with redundant shades of brown. So much so that I could no longer see that forest for the trees. I was simply at a loss to understand what was going on and George Heron's next call added to my dilemma and angst.

"Hi, buddy boy, this is your uncle George and what I have to tell you will rock your world. By the way, it did ours. Are you sitting down with your donut at the ready?"

That was certainly a dramatic opening and I didn't look forward to what my friend might say. I wasn't sure how many more unpleasant surprises I could endure without going absolutely nuts.

"We just received the final test results on the hairs we collected from Ms. Ambrose's casket. Here's what we can definitively tell you about them. As mentioned, they are not human. But they're not animal or synthetic in origin either. In sum, we don't know what they are or where they are from. The DNA strands are unlike anything we've seen before. Harry, I hope you're not playing a prank on us by planting them in the coffin. That would be a no-no and a serious crime."

I assured him I hadn't and he continued with his report of the findings.

"The chromosomal, genetic makeup suggests the hairs are somewhat related to a reptile; not an exact match, but fairly close. They are actually more skin-like structures than hairs. We can't even guess as to the genus of the creature because there's nothing in our database to even point us in a direction. If that's the case, there's a dinosaur roaming the streets of your fair Westlake, my good friend."

I was sitting down while taking in what George just said. My God, could this case get any more bizarre? Yes, it could because the next shoe in this docudrama was about to drop directly in my lap.

***

By best accounts from the medical examiner, Susie Miller, was in bed eating a candied egg. She choked on a piece causing her to vomit bile which she aspirated into her lungs resulting in a heart attack followed by a quick death. The coroner ruled her death to be an accidental one; a tragic one, but accidental nonetheless. Her parents discovered her lifeless body the next morning. I caught her passing in the obits section of the Gazette and felt a great sadness, remembering a pretty, young girl celebrating her birthday on a sunny morning in late August. I thought nothing more of Susie until the following weekend. That's when my world came crashing down once again. I thought my sanity was wearing too thin and worried about my state of mind. I also greatly fretted that I was heading toward a major, emotional meltdown.

***

The call came directly to my home a little after sunrise and woke me from a troublesome sleep. It was the director of the Westlake Community Cemetery. I remembered I'd given him my business card on which I scribbled my home number. I was still groggy from my sketchy dreams; perhaps nightmares would be a more accurate descriptor. He related that there had been another desecration of a grave belonging to one Susie Miller whose remains had only been interred a few days before. I mentally cringed as I absorbed the news. *Here we go again*, I thought.

His description of the scene matched that of the Lucy Ambrose case. It was the same modus operandi at hand or MO as we said in cop jargon. I contacted George Heron and gave him the good news that his forensics team would be gainfully employed awhile longer with Westlake's crime spree. He was not happy with the news.

'Opinions are like assholes because everyone has one,' so the crude saying goes. I had one and it was a big one. One quick check would bolster it or not. And I opined correctly as it turned out. Mr. Rumples had been the master of ceremonies at both Lucy Ambrose's and Susie Miller's birthday parties! I had finally established a nexus between the two crimes and I thought it a good one. There would no longer be any hobos, aliens, bears or people beaming up to heaven on my suspect list. It was Mr. Rumples and he alone.

With my focus exclusively on Mr. Rumples, I could now get back to what I was pretty good at: detecting. I started my research by searching Rumples, clowns, magicians, and the like, online. It turned out that Mr. Rumples had a website and that was how he advertised his service. It was also the way he collected his fees by using a PayPal link. He was very clever in this regard since his customers couldn't trace him or their money. Once established in a community, his performances alone would advertise his exploits by word of mouth. Yes, Mr. Rumples was a devious character whose business would never be rated by the BBB or local authorities.

I could find no mention where his business or he resided; no street address, telephone number or email account could be found. I went so far as to check with the local utility companies for recent customer hook-ups in the area and came up empty handed. Mr. Rumples didn't seem to exist on paper or databases, only in my mind and those of the children he entertained. He was an enigma inside a riddle. I had a challenge on my hands and I'd have to determine his comings and goings the old fashioned way, by surveilling his movements.

The surveillance was a fairly easy and straightforward exercise, as such things go. Just keep tabs on his whereabouts and see what gelled. Oh sure, easy-peasy as they say. But I couldn't have foretold where my investigation would ultimately lead me, even in my wildest dreams.

Mr. Rumples, what an odd name, even for a clown. I thought clowns had catchier names like Bozo or Krusty or Chuckles or Giggles or whatever, but not Mr. Rumples. But that's just my opinion, and since I try to avoid clowns like the plague I'm really not up to speed on the etymology of such things.

Discovering where and when Mr. Rumples would emerge was an easy task. I visited the Westlake Elementary School, the only elementary school and simply asked around. It didn't take long to learn that his next performance would be held at Amy Potter's house next Thursday at 4 pm sharp. I planned to be there as a dutiful, single parent of an imaginary child. I'd be able to easily blend in with the other parents and keep a close eye on Mr. Rumples, not so much his performance, but where he went afterwards.

As expected, Mr. Rumples promptly began his act at 2 pm. Punctuality must have been one of his strong traits, certainly not his dexterity, or lack thereof, in pulling rabbits from hats. But I politely clapped at his antics like everyone else in the audience. Like before, the kids were awestruck by his performance.

The show closed and I watched as Mr. Rumples collected his props and put them into a large, battered suitcase. He then ambled off with an uneasy gait until he reached the bus stop at the corner. I observed him eventually catching the Number 2 bus. I knew its route by heart and discreetly tailed it until Mr. Rumples exited in a rundown section of town. The area was littered with warehouses and commercial buildings; some occupied and operating and some not. The area he walked through was especially seedy and the locus of petty crimes by and against the homeless.

I passed him and took up a position a couple of hundred yards ahead of him and his trajectory. I had no trouble identifying him, given his almost hobbled walking where his body shifted noticeably to the left and right as he approached my location. He looked like a penguin far from its native home.

A couple of minutes later I could discern his destination as it stood alone among the other buildings. It was the Durfey's Wholesale Meats plant that had been in continuous operation for better than 80 years. It was also the town's biggest employer so there were few complaints of the stench wafting from it when the winds were just right. I'd been employed there during college breaks and can confirm the aromas emanating from it were just plain offal.

The plant was old, but several renovations had been made to it over the years as operations expanded and more space was needed to keep up with increased demand for the company's products. It was a prosperous enterprise with its meats being distributed throughout the greater Pittsburgh region. Even the descendents of the original founder still resided in Westlake.

I followed Mr. Rumples to the side of the building and watched him from a distance silently and quickly slip through a door. He must have had a key, but maybe he was a true, talented prestidigitator after all. I waited about 30 seconds or so and tried opening the door. It was locked. No problem, I used my lock gun and I was inside in less than 15 seconds. I spotted Mr. Rumples walking toward the far end of the main plant, pull up what appeared to be a manhole cover, enter, pull down his suitcase and disappear into a large opening. The cover was then put back in place from below.

I guessed the opening was used to collect any runoff of blood from the processing. I moved to the opening, but didn't remove the cover. I wasn't ready to confront Mr. Rumples or tip my hand just yet. But I'd just found Mr. Rumples lair or bolt hole or his home. It didn't make any difference to me what he called his abode. I now had the creep and he was mine for the taking!

I needed help to keep Mr. Rumples under surveillance since I couldn't do it alone. I enlisted the aid of Jim Rainey, a young patrolman I had mentored since he joined the force. He was also a wannabe detective so it was easy to sign him up for the assignment. I briefed him on the case and he was amazed with my findings so far. Of course, he was easily impressed at his age. Me less so, but I believed we had a prime suspect in our sights.

My visit to the town planning office yielded the building plans for Durfey's Wholesale Meats. The structural drawings revealed tunneling beneath the building to facilitate the flow of steam to heat the plant during Westlake's cold winter months. The coal-fired boilers had been abandoned many years ago, but the tunnels remained intact. The town planner guesstimated they covered about 1,000 yards in total length, but they snaked every which way creating a crazy quilt maze under the concrete floors. Mr. Rumples had many places to hide in the tunnels and ferreting him out of his hidey hole might be difficult.

***

It was Halloween eve and the townspeople were filing and flowing into Grove Stadium in large numbers. The high school football field could comfortably hold about 2,000 spectators in its tiered bleachers. However, only the south section of bleachers was open to the public so they could view the large stage that had been erected at midfield. The stadium had been named for Chester Grove, a graduate and local football hero who lost his young life in Iraq some years ago.

The stage was an imposing one, about 40 tall at its maximum height. That was the length of the curtains that covered the façade of the stage. Stand poles of lighting had been placed at the corners of the stage since nightfall came much earlier this time of the year. Large speakers had been placed at the far corners as well to accommodate the public address system. The two massive bonfires, waiting to be lit, flanked the sides of the stage. All in all, it was an impressive construction paid for with taxpayer monies. But no one would complain because the Halloween event was a time honored, welcome spectacle enjoyed by old and young alike.

The mayor opened the show by mouthing the perfunctory words that everyone had heard before. And that was OK with the audience since it was simply part of the expected, traditional pageantry of the holiday. As the mayor began his speech, the two bonfires were lit and the smell of the burning oak and beech mingled to create a familiar, welcoming odor. The crowd enthusiastically applauded the ceremony knowing that the fires would build to a crescendo and light the area around the stage in an eerie, orange glow.

The ritual added to the spooky aura that everyone looked forward to. At the end of his spiel, the mayor needlessly reminded everyone that his Ace Hardware franchise was having a witch of a sale to celebrate Halloween; ten percent off every item in the store. A few people laughed at his ill-timed pitch and pun. The mayor was nothing if not a shrewd businessman and shameless, self-promoting asshole. And that's why he kept getting elected to office.

As to Mr. Rumples, neither I nor Jim Rainey had observed any suspicious behavior. We alternated as his minders and stayed awake with Thermos coffee and large doses of No-Doze. His only venturing from the meat plant was a visit to the UPS store in downtown Westlake. It appeared he had taken out a mail box and we wondered what incriminating correspondence might be residing inside. We'd check that lead out later.

The first act of the Halloween show was the costume contest. Kids, and a few adults, paraded down the steps of the stage and filed past the bleachers so everyone could get a close look at their garb. Witches, ghosts, goblins, space aliens, superheroes and other creatures of unknown origin strutted in front of their parents, friends, relatives and strangers. The scene sort of resembled a catwalk routine by high fashion models on a runway in Paris or Milan, but without the sensuality. The contestants lined up on the stage to be judged by Mr. Mayor who officiated. A small, green hobgoblin won first prize, a Michael Jackson look-alike placed 2nd, and a tall Frankenstein monster captured the 3rd spot. The winners would have bragging rights with their photos displayed in the next issue of the Gazette. It was all good fun and the mayor announced that all the costumes were winners in his judicious opinion.

Next on the schedule were the dancing skeletons that performed to the tune of *Dem Bones*. They cavorted around the stage and hammed it up for the crowd. The florescent bones hand painted on the foreground of their black bodysuits was very imaginative and clever on their parts. I really enjoyed their performance until the 4th rendering of the song and dance routine. They should have stopped after 3 rounds. But the audience loved them and stood up and applauded the performers. I did the same.

But the true apex of the tonight's performance was none other than Mr. Rumples, the clown who had stolen the hearts and minds of the people of Westlake, Pennsylvania. How he could have become a super celeb in a few short months was beyond my comprehension and understanding. He simply wasn't a particularly talented clown or magician, but there was a certain something, a magnetism or charisma, that the kids and adults resonated with and moved towards when he performed. It was he that everyone awaited with rapt attention to his entrance. It was show time, folks!

From behind the curtains, the PA system amplified his voice: "I'm Mr. Rumples, a magician extraordinaire. Watch closely for my tricks and don't have a care. I'm all kiddies pal, best friend of the young. Come to my magical world and enjoy the fun!"

The flute played the strange, ephemeral and haunting song that I'd heard before, but this time the song intertwined with his ditty. How he could do that was unknown to me, but it was an amazing confluence of sound and word. Perhaps it was a recording. Yes, that would neatly explain it.

The curtains then opened and the crowd went wild. Mr. Rumples was standing center stage, highlighted by twin spotlights at his feet. And people were on their feet chanting "Mr. Rumples, Mr. Rumples" over and over again as their faces glowed with joy and adulation. Mr. Rumples simply flapped his long right sleeve in the air to calm them down, suggesting they should be seated. He seemed to be impatient as though he couldn't wait to get started. And that certainly turned out to be correct, much to everyone's shock.

Mr. Rumples began to speak in a loud, commanding, basso profundo voice without the aid of a microphone. It turned out that one wasn't necessary to send his obscene, blasphemous message to the mankind of this world.

"I am called Brussius, spawn of the Devil and loyal servant to my beloved lord of the underworld. Bow down before me, you miserable humans, or suffer my wrath! I reveal my true self to your kind to tell you that each of you is damned to suffer for all eternity for forsaking my master, Lucifer."

The audience recoiled in utter shock and disbelief at what he said. I received the words more as a telepathic communication to my brain rather than aurally. I supposed others in the bleachers heard them in the same manner. People were awestruck, confused and frightened. A pall of fear had fallen over the stadium and, for the most part, the spectators were totally silent. I noticed only a few flashes from cell phone cameras, despite the magnitude of this absolutely bizarre turn of events. My eyes shifted back and forth between the Halloween revelers and Mr. Rumples, trying to take in everything at once.

As I did so, I noticed Mr. Rumples transform himself in front of my very eyes and I couldn't believe what I was now seeing before me.

He discarded his clothing like a snake quickly shedding its skin; actually, he was physically dissembling before us. As he did so, he immediately grew in stature to a height of roughly 10 feet. His (or its) body was very muscular, especially powerful in its upper torso. Its skin took on a mottled gray/green hue without any suggestion of body hair. But, oh God, it was its face that appalled and disgusted me the most.

I admit I couldn't believe what I was seeing. It was much too much horror and madness for my mind to absorb and process. I thought I might be hallucinating under the stress of trying to solve the crimes. Maybe that accounted for my current fugue, and perhaps the racing thoughts of ghouls and demons running through my consciousness. I wasn't interested in parsing the difference between the two at the moment since I was attempting to hold on to what was left of my very tenuous sanity.

Its face was gruesome and I had difficulty staring at it, although I was strongly drawn to it just the same. Its large head sat atop drooped shoulders. The forehead protruded from its skull like our prehistoric ancestors and that gave the freakish creature a brutish look. Its sunken eyes burned like hot coals and I could see bulbous projections on either side of his upper face. No, they weren't horns, but perhaps immature protrusions that might be headed in that particular direction. Its mouth was shaped like a large O with sharp, pointed teeth shaped in V's, ala Mr. Rumples. Even in my worst nightmares, I couldn't conjure up such a monster. Its visage scared the shit out of me and nothing before in my life had frightened me more. But more terror was about to come our way.

"I have lived from time immemorial. My father sent me to your pathetic world to watch and wait for the end times. I have been patient for countless millennia and obeyed my father's edict, but now those times are upon you. You humans are nothing more than rotting flesh. It's your souls that matter to my lord, the one and only true god. Lucifer alone is your savior and salvation, unlike the false gods you have blindly followed. Where are they now?

Oh, but your flesh serves a unique purpose to my father's beloved children. The young bodies of your mortal children fill our stomachs and feed our souls in ways you can't dream of. Enough of these one-at-a-time offerings! My brethren are hungry! You must sacrifice your young to Satan if you wish to save your souls from eternal torment!" He laughed in a high pitched, hideous tone as he spoke the mocking words.

With that, Brussius, or Mr. Rumples if you prefer, slowly and dramatically raised its leathery wings from its sides like a magician opening and unfurling his cape. Its wings were massive, easily dwarfing its large body. There were hands, no not hands, but large claws, appended to the tips of the wings. The ghoul then ascended in flight, slowly hovered over the assemblage, swooped down and snatched the blond hair of a young girl sitting in the bleachers. It then carried its prey upward, toward the moon; a witch's moon on this all hallows eve.

The audience sat stunned and silent, mesmerized at Mr. Rumple's final, and perhaps finest, performance in the town of Westlake, Pennsylvania. No one stirred for a few minutes as each absorbed what they had just witnessed. I finally regained my composure and sketchy sanity and rushed to my car. I knew exactly where Mr. Rumples was going and I planned to confront him or it at home. It wouldn't be a pleasant, sociable house call by any means.

I went lights and siren to the meatpacking plant. I'd finally had my chance to use them, but wished it was another time and place that didn't involve a nasty ghoul. I skidded into the parking lot and grabbed my Mag-Lite and 12 gauge, Remington 870 pump shotgun from the trunk. I then circled the building looking for Jim Rainey. I signaled him a few times with my flashlight, but with no response. That wasn't like Jim, my eager beaver, junior colleague who never shirked his duties. However, I couldn't wait to search for him as time was of the essence because a little girl's life was at stake.

I wasted no time breaching the door lock and ran to the manhole cover I'd seen Mr. Rumples lower himself into earlier. Along the way, I had to sidestep beef carcasses hanging from hooks on the conveyor belt. I pried the cover open and aimed my flashlight down the hole. Calcutta, it seemed, wasn't a black hole by comparison. Everything was an inky black and the noxious smell from the tunnel below nauseated me. I gagged a couple of times before descending down a makeshift ladder.

The steam tunnel was circular in shape and roughly 5 feet in diameter. I was able walk mostly upright if I hunched over. I had no clue as to which direction to proceed in order to locate Mr. Rumples' lair. I mentally flipped a coin and headed off in one direction, thankful there was only dried blood on the floor. So far, the only remarkable things I encountered on my journey in this vile abattoir were skeletons of small animals, maybe rat or cat bones, but certainly nothing of a ghoulish nature. I shone my light down the smaller side tunnels and didn't observe any disturbances to the floor or sides of them. No drag marks, no hoof or footprints, no nothing as far as I could tell. I wondered if Brussius had cloven hoofs and that's why I checked for them.

Jeez, my imagination was really over the top at this point. But given what I saw at the football field, anything was now possible in my mind. My usually logical, well-ordered reasoning had been traumatized to the point that I wasn't sure I could discern fact from fiction anymore.

I decided to reverse direction to examine the other end of the main tunnel. As I did, I noticed a faint light coming from one of the side tunnels. I followed the light and found its source. It came from a rather large dome shaped room that probably held the coal-fired boilers that heated the plant at one time. The light wasn't strong enough to illuminate the entire room so I used my flashlight to peer into its dark, hidden nooks and crannies. I noticed smaller pipes entering and exiting the concrete room and speculated they were water pipes that had once connected the boilers to the coal-fire operation above ground. But what I saw next brought me to my knees, both figuratively and literally, shocking me to the very core of my very being!

The expression about blood running cold was not only a literary device, but a physiological fact I learned by firsthand experience that evening. My head was spinning and I suspected I was having a heart attack or, more likely, a full-blown panic attack.

My mind reeled as my Mag-Lite caught the images of large, transparent containers holding fetuses and placenta. They were neatly stacked, one next to another, on shelves along one of the room's far walls. I continued to scan the room and what I found was even more hideous and gruesome.

As I unsteadily stood, I could see miscellaneous body parts and indescribable viscera piled high on a worktable in the center of the room. It was Mr. Rumples' dining room by the looks of it. It was then I lost it. *It* was my lunch and perhaps my breakfast as well. The vomit spewed from my mouth onto the floor and I wiped off my face with the back of my hand. As I did, I heard a low mewling sound coming from my right and spun my light towards it. I was taken further aback once again if that was possible.

A small child, a girl, of perhaps seven years was sitting in a corner and rocking herself back and forth while making that eerie sound. Her eyes were fixed to some point in space that I couldn't fathom. Even though she saw me, she didn't speak. She was mute and in deep shock. As I approached her, I heard a roar, yes roar is the only way I can describe it. Brussius, the ghoul, or Mr. Rumples the clown-cum-magician, had found me out.

"How dare you violate my sanctuary, you insignificant being?" the monster or thing or whatever loudly boomed. Its voice reverberated throughout the room and pierced my eardrums and I felt the trickle of warm blood coming from my right one. I noticed the child had not reacted in any way. She was still lost, but safe in her self-protecting, emotional cocoon.

"Your kind is an inquisitive bunch; foolish, but still with sensate, inquiring minds. No matter, it's the taste of your young that I seek and relish. And there's no dearth of such delicacies in your world."

Before it could say another word, I leveled my shotgun at its midsection and pulled the trigger. I did so once again. I couldn't miss from this short distance even though my arms were shaky. The #4 buckshot would stop a large bear in its tracks at this range, but not so for a large, angry ghoul. It howled in pain and backed up a few feet, but I'd only wounded it and maybe only slightly. Dropping my shotgun, I quickly scooped up the child into my arms and ran for our lives toward the ladder.

I could hear the pounding of the creature's feet or hooves behind me. Given its enormous size, it seemed to be having difficulty negotiating the confines of the tunnel. And that gave me an advantage that I greatly appreciated. As I pushed the little girl through the hatch opening, I gave her a sharp slap on her butt, hoping she would awake like Sleeping Beauty. But this was no fairy tale. I then screamed to her to run for the door.

The next and last sensation and remembrance I had was the tugging on my legs drawing me back into the tunnel.

***

My new home away from home wasn't too bad considering my current circumstances. It had most of the comforts of my real home, except for one very important thing: my freedom. You see, I've been the guest of the Alleghany Medical Institute for better than a year as best I could tell. Time and time-telling get a little murky after a steady diet of Thorazine and other psychotropic drugs whose names I couldn't even pronounce, much less spell. I've had plenty of time to write this story of Mr. Rumples when I'm lucid enough to do so. The institute's highfalutin name was a bit misleading since most people referred to it as the insane asylum or, more commonly, the nuthouse.

My shrinks labeled my condition as severe depression accompanied by intermittent psychotic breaks from reality. It was sort of like paranoid schizophrenia, but with more words. The doctors were certain of the diagnosis because they had looked it up in their bible. In this instance, that meant the DSM-V; and that was that and nothing more. But I was less certain. I still believed what I saw and experienced at the football stadium and afterwards was real.

The medical experts claimed I was delusional at the time and experiencing one of those psychotic breaks they liked to remind me of from time-to-time. I was still skeptical and cynical of the diagnosis and told them so. They then promptly added the words paranoia, skepticism and cynicism to my list of disorders. I couldn't win for losing with these guys.

I watched the large screen TV in the day ward and was occasionally permitted to use the computer, but always under the watchful eyes of my warders. They weren't in the least surprised that I searched the internet for every bit of information regarding ghouls, demons, goblins, devils and other supposed mythical creatures. After all, those things were my obsession du jour. And I didn't disappoint them. I knew they would note my searches in my chart, but I simply didn't care.

Here's what I can tell you about my Halloween eve experience after I woke up later outside the meatpacking plant. I was disoriented, mentally confused and walked around the plant until my odd, suspicious behavior was reported to the cops. At the station, I babbled on about Mr. Rumples and my experiences right down to the confrontation with the ghoul in the large room below the plant's floor. They fed me coffee and a half box of Krispy Kreme donuts to calm me down, although their expressions and questions suggested they didn't believe my story one wit. I even caught one of my colleagues circle his ear with his finger when he thought I wasn't looking. Well, maybe I was crazy.

I was taken for a psych evaluation at the Alleghany Community Hospital in Pittsburgh. I must not have passed the exam with flying colors since I was immediately shipped off to the institute for further evaluation and treatment. Treatment, at least in my case, was a misnomer unless you counted all of the medical cocktails, injections and IVs containing God only knew what! I was too far gone for simple talk therapy and, besides, what else could I talk about other than ghouls?

***

Naturally, I closely followed the Halloween eve performance at the stadium by reading the Gazette and picking up snippets of information online. The whole cloth stories were transparent and wholly inaccurate in a number of respects. Political spin was running rampant to cover the asses of town officials and to soothe the angst and emotional discomfort of the folk who were present at the event. The official report of their finding's first assertion attempted to explain away Mr. Rumples' amazing, unbelievable, onstage transformation: mass hysteria and/or a brilliant magical feat were the answers. Most likely, it was a combination of both phenomena according to the experts.

The report correctly stated that the audience was emotionally keyed up and anxious for Mr. Rumples to open his act. Psychologists hired by the town's counsel confirmed that conditions were ripe for mass hysteria. Of course, that didn't explain how all of the photos taken by cell phones ended up blurry. But the report did note that the hysteria was exacerbated by the large paper Mache statue of a demon on the stage that did resemble the latter Mr. Rumples. It was built by the high school art classes as a Halloween project. I saw a photo of it and reluctantly allowed that its presence could have contributed to the mass hysteria theory.

Lastly, the report stated that the statue of the demon had been rigged to "fly" across the stage when its ropes were pulled. I didn't disagree that it had been designed from the outset to fly, but it certainly wasn't what I observed that fateful night. What I saw was real and really repulsive.

Jim Rainey hadn't shown up for work. His superiors simply assumed he had flown the coup, ditto for Mr. Rumples. And no one had seen hide or hair or scale of either of them since the Halloween eve performance. The Gazette went so far as to write an article about Mr. Rumples' absence and mourned the fact that he must have moved on to greener pastures

Yep, those were the naïve words the paper used to describe his disappearance. As to Jim, the pundits noted that he was a millennial, those who hopped jobs as frequently as they changed their underwear. He'd eventually contact the department when he needed a job reference. Or so it was thought, but I knew better. Jim had died a horrible death at the hands, or I should say sharp claws, of Mr. Rumples. Still, I guess my crazy accusations had saved the town despite themselves. Mr. Rumples had apparently decided that the town had gotten too hot even for him.

As to the little girl I believed I had saved, she was reported to be slowly recovering from her ordeal, but her prognosis wasn't good. She was still comatose, traumatized by unknown things that reverberated through her closed mind. The authorities claimed she must have wandered off during the performance, unbeknownst to her parents. When they realized she had gone missing, they immediately conducted a frantic search of the stadium grounds without finding her.

They then visited the police department and filled out a missing person report along with a plea to find their daughter as quickly as possible. The weather had turned cool and they greatly feared for her safety. The cops put out a pro forma APB and hoped for the best.

At least the cops followed up on my story about the tunnel and room and confirmed that I had, in fact, been there. That was at least something. They found my shotgun in the large room and were puzzled as to how I'd been able to bend its barrel into a 90 degree angle. There were also two shell casings ejected from my shotgun as well. Otherwise, they found nothing untoward in the room. My shoe prints were the only ones present. There were no glass containers, body parts or other evidence of a ghoulish or criminal nature. The place was clean, maybe too clean in a sense.

So no one believed in my story about a ghoul who was tormenting the world by feeding off young humans. It was all too absurd and fantastical for belief. I agreed it was unbelievable, but it was true and I was terribly frustrated and angry that I couldn't convince anyone. My occasional vitriolic outbursts and violent protestations fell on deaf ears. That's when the straightjacket went on.

***

Most of my endless, hazy days consisted of mindless television programs, apropos of my medical condition. Sometimes a program switched in mid-transmission to a black and white show featuring my new, best friend Mr. Rumples. His message was obviously meant for me and me alone. Others in the day room didn't seem to notice or care about the programming change. Why would they? They were all terminally crazy and most couldn't correctly count the fingers on one hand. But their constant drooling spoke volumes.

Mr. Rumples teased and chided me with his mocking messages. He sometimes did a magic trick or two to simply irritate me. Often he succeeded. He also sung his signature song over and over again in my head: "I'm Mr. Rumples, a magician extraordinaire"

My obsessive mind constantly replayed the tune to the point that I often requested a sedative to calm my jangled nerves. The incessant, never-ending ditty was driving me mad! But how could that be? I was already mad as a hatter so maybe I was moving even further to total, irreversible madness. Were there stages or degrees of madness?

I didn't know or care since I was out to lunch, out of my mind or whatever expression one could apply to my situation. I actually welcomed that at this stage of my life, hoping such a condition would put me out of my misery once and for all. Unfortunately, my keepers didn't allow sharp objects to be around me so I couldn't resolve my misery on my own. Suicide would have been a blessed relief. I wasn't Catholic so I didn't worry about committing a mortal sin. I believed my soul was already the property of Mr. Rumples.

But Mr. Rumples' message was loud and clear enough though; he or it let me live for the sheer pleasure of tormenting me. It was a simple, straightforward message. There was no ambiguity or misunderstanding about it. I was destined to be his (its) human joy toy and personal punching bag for the rest of my natural life. I greatly worried about my afterlife too. May God forgive the many youthful, thoughtless, nasty and mean spirited things I had said and done while on this planet. I had lived a selfish, agnostic life. I offered up a big mea culpa and all of the religiosity that went along with it. I was now a repentant sinner in the eyes of our Lord Jesus. I hoped it wasn't too little too late because I would be damned to Hell otherwise. All thanks to Mr. Rumples, a kids' pal and best friend.

***

The short article in the back pages of the Pittsburgh daily paper caught my immediate attention. A mortuary in Altoona, Pennsylvania had reported a break-in over the past weekend. The body of a young girl, waiting embalming, had been eviscerated with most of her entrails deposited on her chest. The medical examiner described that the remaining organs showed evidence of chewing, along with teeth marks in the flesh. Moreover, the police collected a number of strange hairs or fibers at the scene and were presently trying to identify them.

I didn't bother to report the story to the Westlake Police Department since I would again be ridiculed and dismissed by my former colleagues and friends as a crazy person; and that was a pretty accurate assessment of my present state of health. But I strongly believed that Mr. Rumples had moved on to greener pastures as the Gazette presciently observed many months ago. He (it) had found a new feeding ground to explore and exploit to his or its own, perverse ends. And one of those ends was the devouring of young, human flesh. Capturing a soul or two along the way was simply an added bonus.

Such things were no longer my concern.

Not again.

Not yet.

Others could pursue these cases, but not me. I was sleeping very well these days thanks to my strong meds. No longer did I have nightmares about demons or ghouls. Fortunately, I had no more dreams or hopes about anything or anyone, including myself. The old Harry Balt ceased to exist, but somewhere, deep inside my foggy limbic system, a new, mightier persona was forming. One that would someday soon be *cured* and *normal* in the eyes of my shrinks. This new and improved Harry Balt would find a way to iron out all the wrinkles so that Mr. Rumples, the demonic clown, wouldn't have the last laugh after all.

What Lies Beneath Wraithfall Ruins

Daniel Hunter

What Lies Beneath Wraithfall Ruins
Daniel Hunter

The holy warrior climbed the face of the white-capped King's Mountain, so-named in honor of the line of ruling kings of Shandwick. The peaks were enveloped in a thick, wintery fog, made visible by the light of the pale moon. In spite of the near-vertical climb and the frigid, blowing snow, his steel determination helped him overcome the unforgiving elements.

The Black Knight lived up to his name. In stark contrast to his white environment, he wore forge-black armor, a solid black, wolf-skinned cloak, with an onyx-encrusted scabbard hanging off his back and a black, knife-toting bandolier around his chest.

The cold stung bitterly, seeking his skin through the metal armor and radiating down to his bones. Though his gear generally proved protective, it ill-prepared him for his current endeavor. Still, he appreciated its strength if not its weight against the cutting winds. Each labored breath vented plumes through the three vertical slits of his horned helmet's face guard. Each breath was crucial, but the high altitude made it near-impossible.

The wind's fury slowed his progress even more, requiring him to pace his ascent to the lull between gusts. Just as he began to doubt his own tenacity, he glanced the quiet, secret monastery just up ahead, at the mountain's apex. He watched as a black raven – the first sign of life he'd seen in hours – circled the monastery, daring to fly the currents of the angry howling wind. His goal in sight, even the weight of his armor coated with a thin sheen of ice wouldn't be enough to stop him.

He had good reason for his struggles.

A sinister force was after him.

It would soon find him if he wasn't careful.

Evasion was his life of late– moving only during the darkest of night, somehow succeeding where so many others had failed.

The rocky cliff-side flattened out dramatically, allowing him to climb forward rather than up for a short distance. Finally the angle became manageable enough to permit him to rise up and walk across the white, rocky ground until reaching the cobblestone steps that led to the monastery doors.

Flanking the large, oaken doors were large granite statues, each one featuring a martyred saint from the past – Saint Gideon the Meek on one side, and Saint Elijah the Unyielding on the other.

Despite the simplicity of both men, no more than peasants back when they walked the earth, the statues were carved and created as they might appear in the heavenly realms, long, flowing angelic wings on their backs stretched out and upward toward the celestial sky, and a look of stern compassion was captured by the sculptor.

It made the saints appear wise and benevolent. The one on the right held a large stone book in its hand while the other held a chalice lifted heavenward.

"As your will allows, oh Creator," the Black Knight whispered, bowing his head and taking a knee before the monastery, partially to catch his breath but primarily out of reverence.

For a moment he could feel the presence of his God in the air, reminding him that the black void after his soul was far from the monastery – he was allowed a brief moment of rest. For now at least. His dark pursuer wouldn't always be kept at bay. The day of reckoning would come.

The raven glided down and landed on the book of Saint Gideon, curiously watching the praying knight.

The knight rose to his feet, approached the doors and banged on the right-hand portal, dislodging a shower of snow. Evidently no one had come or gone since before the wintry storm. He waited patiently until the large wooden double doors began to open, revealing a crack of light and a much-needed gust of warmth escaping from inside the monastery. The black raven flew swiftly through the crack the moment the doors opened.

A man with a grey wispy beard hanging down to his chest popped his head out and squinted, letting his eyes adjust from the well-lit torches of the monastery to the darkness of the night, ducking just in time as the raven sailed by.

"Blast it, Aidenn! Cursed raven," he said, swatting futilely long after the raven passed through.

His humble brown robe was practical, well-worn at its hem from dragging across the floor, with only a belt made from camel hair to keep it cinched in place. Each line upon his wizened face bespoke a wealth of experiences as readily as the rings on an ancient tree. He blinked rheumy eyes in an attempt to focus the features of the black silhouette standing in front of him. Finally, with the realization of who the knight at his door was, a large smile lit his face and provided a brief spryness to his step as he pulled the door open and rushed forward.

"My, my! He has returned, still alive!"

They did not know each other well, but this wasn't the first time the Black Knight had entered. This was his third visit, and with each stay he received wise council from both the enormous library and the man known as Byron the Wise.

A smile hidden by his helm returned his sentiment of affection.

"Hello, teacher. It is good to see you. The darkness has yet to swallow me, thanks be to the Almighty."

Byron looked past the Black Knight with grave concern. "Quickly, quickly! Come in, and make haste."

As the dark warrior entered the monastery, the old man quickly closed the door behind him and barred it with a thick slab of wood.

"I was worried you would not be able to find the monastery again, but it seems the Lord God provided you a way."

"Indeed He did. He always has a way of opening the veil of mist at the last minute and providing illumination. Are there any other Knights of the Word in the monastery?"

"I'm afraid not. It's been over a year since our last student departed. You are the first Knight of the Word we seen since then, and still the only who chooses not to wear the brilliant, shiny chrome armor of your brothers and sisters. Of course, I understand why, but I still think you ought to remain in the light."

"Though dark on the outside, teacher, there is light in my soul. It is perhaps the only reason I remain alive in this world."

"Come," Byron said, rounding the corner of one hall into the next. "Let's find you a room in the dormitory and get you rested."

He noticed the raven watching them as it rested on an empty sconce in the hall as they walked by.

"Thank you, but there is no time. I have come with purpose."

Byron slowed his pace and looked over his shoulder at the knight. "Oh?"

He nodded. "The catacombs."

The Wise One gave him a knowing look. "You mean the library. Not the sacred library above ground, but the *secret* library underneath the catacombs."

"I have discovered that even secrets have secrets – just as there is a hidden library underneath the monastery, there is *even more* to it that we do not know about. That is why I have come."

"You know of the sleeping guardians," he whispered, as if speaking too loud might wake a slumbering adversary.

"I do, but that is where I must go."

Byron stroked his beard for a few long seconds.

"Then I will go with you."

"This is not your fight, teacher."

"Nonsense! You may carry a burden, but I am still an ally, friend, and servant to the Order of the Word."

The Black Knight hesitated. "You are wise, old monk, but your days of battle are long over. Follow me as you will, but I beg you retain your wisdom to avoid pitfalls and troubles underneath the monastery."

The monk gave him a condescending look. "Who thinks he is the teacher now? Yes, yes. You are right. Let us grab provisions, extra torches and a map of the catacombs before we go. This will be more adventure than I have had in years."

***

The raven tried to fly through the open door to the catacombs until Byron drove him back with a lit torch. "Shoo, Aidenn! Back! If you go through these doors we will never find you again."

The torchlight danced its way down the corridor of dark shadows as the two men entered, leaving the door cracked behind them. The Black Knight brushed away cobwebs while Byron used his torch to burn them away in order to better see the path ahead.

They traversed the main level of the crypt, speaking only when necessary out of respect for the sleeping dead. Both offered mental prayers of peace with each sarcophagus, tomb and urn they passed by. With every turn and corner, the Black Knight held the map up to Byron's torch for light, making sure they were proceeding in the right direction so as not to waste time.

Finally they came to the large, dusty stone door leading to the underground library. It took a great amount of effort, but the Black Knight pushed them open to harsh grinding sound of stone against stone.

"The library, just as the map showed," the knight whispered. Byron nodded his agreement.

Leather-bound books covered in centuries of dust and webs lined shelves that stacked in row upon row as far as the eye could see. Various geographical and nautical maps, portraits of clergymen long dead, scenes of battles now forgotten by even the victors adorned the walls, and statues and busts of the holiest of saints filled numerous alcoves.

This was where the map ended – the library itself was unmarked, so it was up to the Black Knight and Byron the Wise to navigate the labyrinth of books.

***

After searching for hours, a cold breeze whistled past the Black Knight. He stopped in his tracks, immediately seeking its source. The gentle draft floated by again, and this time he felt it through the tiny chinks in his armor, through his undershirt and down to his skin, almost as if tapping him on the back of his right shoulder.

He could've sworn there was a word or two carried upon the air as if whispered by a weak breath, but if that was truly the case, he nonetheless couldn't quite make it out.

The knight strained his ears, waiting to hear more, but the breeze had stopped. He looked over at Byron who, judging by his indifferent expression, hadn't noticed.

The Black Knight turned to his right and immediately spotted a large painting on the wall that caught his attention. Somehow it was different from others he had seen.

The unmarked and unnamed painting prominently featured a large hill. A small city rested near its base while a thin layer of faded green vegetation dusted the top of the brown, dusty hill.

There was something about it that fascinated the Black Knight. He studied the scene carefully – each line, each stroke of the artist's brush, and each crevice in the large stony hill.

And then he saw it – a hidden image blended into the side of the mountain.

"A skull," he whispered to Byron, tracing his finger over its features as he saw it on the painting.

"Golgotha?" Byron replied.

"I believe so. The hill they called the skull – the place where Christ was crucified."

The wide-eyed, excited monk brought his face closer, trying to make it out for himself. "I don't believe it! You are right! But there are no crosses on the hill?"

"This must be it." The Black Knight placed his hands against the map, searching for a seam where the wind might have come from, also quite possibly a secret lever or switch. His fingertips finally found a soft depression blended into the painting – right inside the mouth of the skull.

The knight carefully pushed the secret stone button, and the entire section of wall opened up, revealing a hidden room.

"Incredible! You have unearthed a secret passage which may have been hidden since its creation ages ago. It is certain that centuries of monks living in this monastery missed this *astonishing* discovery."

The Black Knight cautiously stepped into the small chamber. At the far end of the room was a stone statue. Time had withered away the features on its face, making it impossible to read its expression. There was nothing etched in stone and no placard to reveal whom the statue was modeled after. It bore a chipped shield in one arm, and with its other hand it held a spear broken in half with the bottom portion missing.

Directly in front of the statue, a dark marble podium held a large, black leather-bound book opened to the center.

He hesitated. Something was off about the room.

Then he saw a feint yellow light slowly glow through the cracks of the statue. It grew in intensity until it seemed it might fracture the statue in its attempt to escape. The light illuminated the entire room, and then just as quickly as it appeared it vanished, plunging the room into darkness.

His attention riveted to the statue, he watched as a softly glowing mist emanated from it and then came together as if reforming. The details were difficult to make out, but while the bottom part was nothing more than featureless vapors, the upper region of the mist-like entity swirled and undulated until it resembled a human-like form with a distinct torso, arms and a head.

Despite all the wonders of the world that the Black Knight and Byron the Wise had witnessed, this was far beyond anything either had ever seen.

The knight wasn't sure if the apparition was friend or foe. It didn't threaten, but it didn't speak, either. His hand remained on the hilt of his sword.

"We have come in search of answers. Will you help us?" he said respectfully, standing ready and waiting for a response.

The mysterious presence spoke so deeply and powerfully that its voice reverberated off the walls:

Does Death frighten you?

The Black Knight wasn't sure if it was a genuine question or a possible threat.

"We all fear death by certain degrees," he said resolutely, despite the foreboding manifestation before him, "but I will accept death only when it is my time, not by my will but by that of my Lord."

Tell me then, if Death chases you why do you run?

For a moment he was taken aback. If the spirit knew about his struggle, then it could likely see into his very soul.

"I do not run for my own sake. There is one last quest I must finish – for that of another. Only then will I allow my fate to run its course."

The spirit stared at the knight as if searching his heart for truth, silent, merely wafting ever so slightly.

The arm of the stone statue moved then, mechanically, with a grinding sound. Its wrist twisted, holding out the broken spear.

You speak with honesty and a noble heart. Therefore, the spear and the book will be yours until your quest is complete.

The spirit faded back toward the statue and dissipated until it was gone.

The knight relaxed slightly, allowing a sag in his tired shoulders and a deep exhale. "Who or what was that?"

"Your guess is as good as mine," the old man said, slightly trembling and looking over his shoulder. "An angel? A saint? Something more sinister? I do not know – but had it been a spirit of ill will, this would have turned out differently."

The knight carefully reached out for the top part of the spear. Upon closer observation, it was a *wooden* spear, unlike the stone statue and its shield, likely added to the statue after its creation. He took it from the statue and examined it in his hands. "This is definitely dated from centuries past. The wood is old, as is the steel tip. The tip of the spear is saturated in dried blood, as is the first length of the shaft."

He tucked the weapon away into his belt and turned to the book on the podium and told the old man, "I do not know why it told me to take the spear – that was unexpected. But somehow the spirit knew that this book is what I came for." The knight ran his hand over the dusty tome, carefully closing it and inspecting the cover.

"Memento Morieris: The Book of the Dead." the knight whispered as he read the title.

"… remember you will die," the old monk translated with horror. "My son, this is a book of great evil. What in the blazes is it doing down here in this holy place? You best put it back. "

"If I only could," he said, opening up the large book again.

If the Black Knight heard him, he wasn't responding. Instead he was studying the book and its contents. "There are pages missing."

"Are you listening? As if that wasn't bad enough, they say this book is the very *opposite* of the Book of Life. The very same Book of Life spoken of in Revelations!

"Revelations 20:12 says, '*And I saw the dead, great and small, standing before the throne, and books were opened. Another book was opened, which is the Book of Life. The dead were judged according to what they had done as recorded in the books.*'

"And then it goes on to say . . ."

The knight interrupted, "*Anyone whose name was not found written in the book of life was thrown into the lake of fire.* I remember the Holy Scriptures."

"Then you must understand that just as the Book of Life contains the names of the saved, the Book of Death – the very tome you hold in your hands – contains the names of the unsaved . . . the *names* of the *damned!*" His bony hands quivered as he spoke, "They are those who will not see eternal paradise, but instead will perish within the flames. The book was not *meant* to be within our mortal hands."

"You are right, yet this is my burden. I wish it were not so. It is also said that this book, through dark secrets of necromancy, reveals the stories of tragedy of those who died before their time – murdered, wronged, or touched by the hand of evil. It is one of those stories that I must discover."

The old man sighed and bowed his head, relenting. "I still think this is a bad idea, but I will support you. Understand, though, that if you are not careful with this, it could *turn* you. Destroy you!"

"You have always been a great teacher. I promise I will heed your warning."

***

There wasn't time to stay and rest. *It* was coming and never slept.

The wise old monk gave him food rations, extra clothing and other supplies for his trip before sending him off. Even the raven watched inquisitively as the Black Knight departed into the cold wintery night, vanishing in the darkness.

"Well, then. All that's left to do is pray, isn't that right, Aidenn?"

The raven swiftly left its perch and flew down the corridor.

"What's gotten into you tonight?" Byron followed the raven, wondering what kind of trouble it was seeking.

After following the raven, it suddenly hit him: "The catacomb doors!" He couldn't remember if he properly sealed them or not, but he was having his doubts. Curse his old age. "Aidenn, wait!"

Byron ran after the raven as fast as his knobby legs would take him, rounding one corner and then the next before realizing that was *exactly* where the stupid bird was heading.

He stepped in the chamber just in time to see the raven fly through the open catacomb door, disappearing into the darkness where he had just returned from.

***

You were nothing more than dust, and soon you shall return. Remember you will die.

The Lost Scriptures of the Book of Hezekiah 3:8

***

"This is a bad idea," the young boy whispered. He was barely a teenager and small for his age.

Dusk was rapidly approaching, and it wouldn't be long until they were forced off the King's Highway and up the mountain pass. The pathway was forbidden by the king, and as such found itself overgrown with tall weeds and sprouting grass coming out of the dirt, slowly winding up the backside of the mountains and deeper into untraveled territory.

"Will you stop whining, Elias?" The only girl of the group of six chastised him harshly without so much as bothering to strain her neck in an effort to turn around. The other four boys only laughed at him.

"You shouldn't have let him come along, Emmeline," the oldest of the group and her boyfriend, Samuel, said.

"'*Lady* Emmeline'," she corrected. Samuel sighed and echoed her response.

"Why do you call her that? That's not even her real name," Hiram, Samuel's closest friend, asked.

Samuel shrugged, but Emmeline snapped at Hiram, "Because I told him too. Do you have a problem with my name all of a sudden?"

This time Hiram was the target of ridicule as the other boys laughed.

Elias trialed the group, not sure of what he was getting himself into. "Say what you will, but the music and dancing took a lot of effort and coordination by the orphanage. We really should think about going back before it's over."

"Ugh. That was the *worst* performer I have ever heard in my life. He couldn't sing a lick," Emmeline complained.

Samuel laughed at Elias, "I don't know what you're complaining about. It's not like you have a girlfriend to dance with like I do."

"Good point. So why aren't you two dancing back at the orphanage?" Elias asked without missing a beat.

Samuel scowled at him, but Emmeline simply tried to put their bickering behind her. "You know why, Elias."

'Lady Emmeline', as she called herself – and made everyone *else* call her – might have been a brat, but she was smart. Incredibly smart. Not only was she born that way, but she'd spend hours upon hours reading every morning, and then in the afternoon concocted great adventures based on the whimsical and fantastic stories she read – fiction or otherwise.

Her latest adventure consisted of finding and retrieving a crown – a *real life* crown – made of the purest gold. It wasn't hard for a beauty like her to find an entourage to adventure with her.

She went on and on about how the crown was once nicknamed 'The Queen's Heaven', named as such after the diamond angel set as the apex of the crown, supposedly watching over its wearer from heaven. The kingdom where the aforementioned queen once ruled had long been destroyed, and some manuscripts dubbed the crown thereafter as 'The Queen's Abandoning'.

Whatever the name, Emmeline didn't care – it was *pure gold* with a *diamond angel* on top!

Elias knew she was looking for trouble. As exciting as she made those adventures seem, her panache for trouble was half of the reason why he went with her – hoping to help keep her *out* of it.

Night was falling, but the six youths were getting closer to their destination. Several of the boys were growing restless, but Emmeline was unwavering in her mission to find that crown.

"Did you know Wraithfall Ruins used to be Wraithfall Castle?" she asked anyone who would listen to her.

Samuel and Hiram didn't appear to care.

Thomas and Tobias were oblivious, frequently looking over their shoulders and wondering how they let her talk them into straying this far from the orphanage. Elias could tell the thoughts of unseen things within the dark curtain of night were creeping into their minds.

Elias answered her, "Of course. Wraithfall Castle was haunted, and some say it was destroyed by the Wrath of God Himself. And now it remains nothing more than haunted ruins."

For the first time all night, Emmeline not only turned around to look at Elias, but she appeared to be genuinely impressed.

He continued, "They *also* say it was a disobedient girl who wandered to the castle in the first place, causing its destruction – and nearly her death." Elias gave a fake cough to get her attention, driving home the huge risk she was taking.

She didn't so much as flinch. "Please. You've been listening to our caretaker too much and her crazy stories. The ruins *aren't* haunted."

Elias continued, "Sure – because the crumbling castle *killed* the phantoms and ghosts, so it's no longer haunted?"

Emmeline was letting her agitation show, but nevertheless Elias could sense she was enjoying the debate. "The castle never *was* haunted, Elias."

"Yeah; that's just stupid," Samuel interjected. Elias smiled when Emmeline threw a snotty glare at Samuel, unimpressed with his simpleton dialogue.

"Books have *recorded* the fact that it was haunted. Remember the Horned Soldiers? The ones that fought an army of flesh and blood? Many of the surviving soldiers of Shandwick testified they fought against the undead of the castle."

"It was also recorded that their so-called opponents were invisible or simply didn't exist. That means no *proof.* No bones, no rotting flesh – nothing."

"Skeptic," he sighed.

"Gullible boy," she quipped back. Despite her harsh words Elias thought he saw the thinnest of smiles on her face out of the corner of his eye.

"So you believe in a crown, but not in the undead?"

"Of course! A crown is *tangible.* I have seen a crown before, as many have, but no one has seen the undead – because they simply do not exist."

"So you don't believe in the White Widow?"

There was a loud snapping of a branch somewhere in the black forest far off the trail.

"*WHAT WAS THAT?*" Thomas shouted, jumping with a start.

Emmeline threw a hand on her hip and shot Thomas a deathly glare, annoyed that their conversation was interrupted, and as a byproduct, ruined.

Elias half expected Samuel to laugh at Thomas, but he didn't.

"Guys, I think we should turn back," Tobias cautiously whispered.

Emmeline stopped, turned around to face the boys, and folded her arms, bringing the group to an abrupt halt.

"Look. Whoever wants to go back, do it now. But *I swear* if the Caretaker finds out about this . . . *Heads. Will. Roll.*"

"I'm . . . not scared, but this is taking much longer than I thought," Tobias said.

"Me too," Thomas quickly added.

"Fine," Emmeline said, brushing them off with the back of her hand, much like an exasperated queen to her irksome servants.

"I think I'm going to head back, too," Hiram interjected. He tried to play it off like he wasn't scared, but Elias could tell otherwise.

Samuel threw him a look of disgust. "You too?"

"Hey! It's not like that. What are the odds we will find a crown? I mean – it is getting late, and the risk is bigger than the reward. I . . . I'm sorry, but . . ."

"Just go with them already! You three be safe, but remember what I said."

"I know, I know," Hiram told her. "We won't say a word."

"This might be a good time for all of us to consider . . ."

"Don't even finish that sentence, Elias*!"* she threatened him. "If you want to leave, then . . ."

"I'm staying, I'm staying!" he quickly said, much to the disappointment of Samuel.

He wasn't quite sure, but it almost looked like . . . relief wasn't the right word. Pleased? No . . . nothing short of a golden crown could possibly *please* the almighty Miss Lady Emmeline.

Glad? She was *glad* that he was staying?

Who could tell for certain? He shrugged it off, knowing he probably misinterpreted her signals, maybe due to the flickering shadows against her face from the dim illumination of Samuel's lantern. It was always hard to tell with her anyway.

"Alright, then. Let's get moving."

Just like that, their group was cut in half.

Samuel shined the lantern on Emmeline's map. He determined they were almost at the top of the mountain and out of the main forest. They should be at the ruins in no time.

"So who's the White Widow?"

Elias and Emmeline looked at Samuel as if he quite possibly just asked the world's stupidest question.

Elias asked, "You haven't heard the legend of the White Widow?"

"Nope." He didn't really seem to care – he seemed to ask only out of boredom.

Emmeline chimed in, "Maybe you've heard of her other names. The Witch Queen of Wraithfall Ruins?"

Samuel shook his head.

She continued, "The Wraith Witch? The White Banshee?"

"Sorry. I'm not into ghost stories," he mocked.

She rolled her eyes and looked at Elias, deplored by Samuel's knowledge – or lack thereof – deliberately ignoring Samuel as if he were no more than a monkey that couldn't understand how possibly deep her grievous disappointment could be.

A slight curve surfaced on the upper lip of Elias. He suddenly felt the first signs of a possible invite into Emmeline's 'club'.

Well . . . assuming he wanted such a thing.

"Should you tell him, or should I, Elias?"

Elias cleared his throat. "The White Widow is the epitome of frightening tales passed down from parents to their children, warning them to stay away from Wraithfall Ruins. That, of course, is where she supposedly lies in wait – trapped somewhere far underneath the confines of the castle."

"You don't believe this nonsense, do you Emmeline?"

"Of course not, Samuel. But I've at least *heard* of the stories."

Elias, as if his very own words were unnerving him, looked over both shoulders before continuing. "Her wails and cries can be heard at night from miles and miles around, they say. All who hear her screams are cursed – permanent insanity or even *death* await those under her sign of ill omen."

Samuel looked up at the night sky, pretending to not let the story unnerve him, but the width of his open eyes gave him away. Emmeline noticed it, too – she actually smiled out of pity for him.

"You said she was trapped underneath the castle? That's not what I heard. *I* heard she roams the forest," Emmeline stated matter-of-factly.

"That's impossible. She was buried alive – sealed inside a tomb."

"What?" It was Emmeline's turn to be alarmed.

"That's what I read anyway."

"Where did you read that?"

"One of the books in the library. I spend a lot of time there."

"I know. I see you in there all the time," she said, but her curiosity was growing. "What else do you know about her?"

"Well, the Queen's Abandoning was originally *her* crown. Supposedly."

"No!"

"Yes. The king gave it to her as a wedding gift, but he was not a good man. Legends say he soon afterward took up with a mistress. He couldn't kill her and lose face with his people, so he made her vanish. Disappear. No one ever saw her again.

"Whispers spoke of him doing the unthinkable. The king walled up and entombed his queen *alive* – in a dungeon somewhere far beneath the castle. They say her cries and screams could actually be heard *through* the walls. She screamed relentlessly, but it was futile

– eventually she died, and her body was never recovered, apparently still entombed in her sealed up prison.

"But here's the interesting part – they only *think* she died. The screams never actually stopped. One day her wailing instantly changed from the most pitiful cries of fear and horror to a sudden, inexplicable and terrible wrath, brimming over with furious anger."

"Why?" Emmeline dared to ask.

"Because the cries of fear were from while she was alive, but the screams of rage were brought forth the moment she died . . . and *turned undead.*

". . . and they never stopped."

He could tell by the way her hands crossed, rubbing up and down her opposite arms, that he gave her the chills. He actually meant to frighten Samuel – and he *did* – but he also unnerved *himself,* recalling such a tragic and horrible story and pondering the horror of what it must have been like to have been entombed alive, shrieking with fear and clawing in desperation as the final brick and mortar were sealed in place.

All three of them were officially frightened.

"Then what," she asked with a slight tremor to her voice, as if embracing the fear that would come with the rest of the story might somehow calm her down by mere knowledge and understanding.

He shrugged. "That's it. That's all I know."

Samuel butted in their conversation. "Wait. If she died, her ghost could've escaped, right? Walked through the walls and all of that?"

Elias thought for a moment. "You know, you have a point. I suppose that is possible. But her bones are still likely somewhere behind the wall."

Samuel's great discovery served to only frighten the three youth even more.

After walking in silence, Emmeline finally spoke. "I heard she haunts the countryside. Not that I believe it! But . . . she has the power to animate death, forcing ancient bones to rise and walk the earth at her will."

She swallowed as she said, "There are other shadows that follow her – maybe ladies of her court, if the White Widow is truly the first queen – and they are *real* evil shadows, absent of bodies or structure, moving about as if they were alive."

She calmly asked, "You don't suppose . . ."

A loud, howling scream from somewhere beyond the dark pine trees pierced the silent night air and echoed across the mountain, forbidding Emmeline from asking her question.

All three jumped, but Samuel screamed louder than the others. Before Elias and Emmeline could blink, Samuel was halfway down the path, running just as fast as his legs could carry him. The light from his lantern grew smaller and dimmer until it vanished altogether, and just like that Samuel was gone.

"You *coward*!!" Emmeline shouted with her fist raised in unabashed defiance. She would have been terribly unnerved herself if she wasn't so upset with her boyfriend. She turned to Elias with her wide-rimmed eyes fixating on him. "That was probably just an old barn owl."

"There aren't . . ."

"Shut up! I *know* there aren't any *barns* around here! Then . . . whatever kind of an owl! That wasn't the White Widow, *Elias*!" She spat his name out with heavy concentration on each syllable – '*E-lie-as*' – as if a youth in trouble by his parents.

"Uh, do we go after him?" Elias dug out his own lantern and tried to light it.

She reluctantly sighed, "Yes, but quickly. This is already taking too long."

After Elias successfully lit the lantern, he and Emmeline tried to chase after Samuel, but they never caught up. His fear proved to be too intense and his head start too great to overcome.

After backtracking for longer than either would've liked, Emmeline finally said, "He's probably caught up with the other three by now, as terrified as he was. Let's go back."

"Wait. After all of this, you still want to go to the ruins?"

She rolled her eyes. "Of course! Why wouldn't I?"

"For one thing, your boyfriend is gone – he completely left you stranded. Secondly, it's doubtful we won't make it back by morning light at this rate."

"If you want to go, I won't stop you." She looked over Elias and pursed her lips. "Actually, I thought you would be the first to run. Guess I was wrong."

Did she just admit she was wrong? It figured no one would be around to witness her admission.

He threw his hands up in defeat. "I'm not leaving you out here alone."

Emmeline stepped closer. Her curious nature was coming out again. "Why did you come in the first place? You never liked me."

"I . . . that's not true," he stammered.

Her hands dropped to her hips. "You're avoiding the question."

That was true. The answer was easy.

Like all the other boys, he liked her. *Really* liked her. Even in spite of her bossy attitude. It was her adventurous side that drew him to her – among other things, of course. It was the way she sought out a challenge, or the fact that she knew a *lot* of information – even if she was the first to tell you so.

But the main reason why he was with her was merely to keep her out of trouble. Nothing good could come from Wraithfall Ruins, and he was worried that this time her adventurous side would prove too much.

He chickened out. "I came because….I don't really like dancing and I had nothing better to do."

Her eyes opened wide and she laughed, clearly not expecting that answer.

"Look. If you want to leave, that's fine. Go ahead. But I'm going."

So much for talking her out of it.

"Then I'm going, too."

His words unexpectedly brought an upward curve to her lips. For the first time that night, Elias witnessed a wonderful smile, so bright that it rivaled the radiance of the moon itself.

***

They say she stole the children, the ones who disobey
And turned them into shadows while the night despairs and woes
Others say she ate the children; the ones who ran away
So flee from Wraithfall Ruins for the truth God only knows
An old forgotten poem of the Province and Land of Shandwick

***

The Black Knight closed the leather-bound book and placed it back within his large traveling sack – one long chapter was enough for now. His vision grew blurry and each word weighed heavier on his soul.

The wise old monk was right. He warned him that the book of damnation had the potential to drive him mad, and he was beginning to experience a small taste of the psychological effects.

No doubt the evil chipped away at his soul. The knight took a knee and began to pray – pray for salvation and the strength to remain strong and steadfast. He prayed for the Lord to keep evil at bay and to let the light prevail.

The Lord heard his prayers, but He wasn't answering quite yet – he didn't feel any better. Standing tall and ready to resume his excursion, the knight knew that the remainder of his journey would prove a great battle of spiritual warfare.

The old stone bridge leading to Wraithfall Ruins – or as some claimed, *the realm of the dead itself* – came into view before him.

With one armored foot in front of the other, the long walk across the old arched stone bridge felt as if it were in slow motion, as if he were walking in place as the long bridge moved underneath his feet. Maybe even backward. The once solid bridge with tall, solid stone rails was strong and mighty at one time, but those days were long past. Each step demanded caution as one wrongly placed foot potentially could cause part of the stone to break away.

The ruins of the castle became visible under the moonlit sky as the Black Knight reached the center of the arched bridge at its apex. He marveled at how only a few surviving walls remained, jutting sharply out of the acres upon acres of rubble.

As he reached the end of the bridge, he caught the flickering of shadows from the dark forest out of the corner of his eye. One shadow in particular stretched out from one of the trees, slowly creeping along the dirt ground. The moment the knight's eyes fell on the elongated shadow, it stopped moving.

He looked up to the sky, noting the moon was on the *same side* of the tree as the shadow – there was no light source on the opposite side to *create* the shadow.

It shouldn't have existed.

The sounds of a rustling in a nearby bush grabbed his attention, causing him to brace himself and wrap his fingers around the hilt of his sword. He listened for a moment, ready to draw steel, but there was nothing more to be heard.

Maybe it was only an animal. Possibly a dead branch – a widow maker – falling from the top of a tree. Perhaps something more, or perhaps nothing at all.

He relaxed his grip and continued his march, looking back to the impossibly abnormal shadow. It was gone – or rather it was back to its normal dimensions, matching that of the shadows next to it.

He questioned his very sanity.

Shadows, he thought to himself.

His past was catching up with him.

Stepping off the bridge, he faced the moon and looked up into its dim blue light.

"*It* is closing in on me, isn't it?" he asked the moon. The pale white orb remained aloof.

"You are playing games with shadows tonight," he told it plainly, even if it wouldn't respond.

Maybe the tome had a bigger impact on his mind than he thought. It was possible he was losing his mind already, flirting with the brink of madness.

"*Shadows, shadows everywhere . . . shadows, shadows in the air,*" he whispered in a singsong voice. It felt as if he were small, a tiny figure trapped inside his own head, being kept inside by knobby clawed fingers extending over him like prison bars covering a dome. He wanted to break free, but the pressure exerted upon him made him feel like he was going to explode in a mass of fluid and matter.

There was something about shadows he was trying to recall, but his brain wasn't cooperating. But he at least *knew* he was going mad. Could one be truly insane if they *knew* they were insane?

He gritted his teeth and began to say the Lord's Prayer over and over inside his head, hoping to restore a shred of sanity. At the very end, he added, *"Lord, grant me serenity. Lord, guide my soul and my mind."*

Maybe the Lord heard him this time, because the fog inside his mind slowly lifted, not altogether vanishing but just enough for him to remember. He opened his eyes, and looking down at the ground while standing in the moonlight he turned around in a full circle. What he expected to see *wasn't there*.

It was true. It was fact, and he remembered.

He was breaking free from the insanity, but this was different – this time it was reality. He finally recollected a long forgotten truth he had subconsciously covered up, deep within the realms of his mind.

The Black Knight had no shadow.

***

"It is a simple matter for the shadow to go forward ten steps," said Hezekiah. *"Rather, have it go back ten steps."*
2 Kings 20:10

***

He wasn't entirely sure that he knew where he was. Byron the Wise didn't dare call it *lost* for the sake of avoiding panic. It was more along the lines of knowing where he was, just with an uncertainly of how to get out of the blasted catacombs.

"I'll cook you for dinner if I get my hands on you, Aidenn," the old monk mumbled as he followed the black raven – his bane and cause of his excursion.

He swore Aidenn was playing a game with him. Each time Byron closed in on the bird, it took off and few away – deeper into the labyrinth.

At last – cornered!

127

Byron chucked with glee as the raven managed to work its way into a dead-end chamber. The room was mostly void except for a single stone sarcophagus adorning the center of the dark room. The lonely coffin was surrounded by two large paintings on each side and a life-sized statue in a dark crescent-shaped alcove on the far side of the room.

Byron was all that stood between the cursed bird and the exit. Moving slowly into the room and taking off his long, brown robe with the purpose of using it as an impromptu net, Byron stared the raven down as it sat quietly on the statue of Saint Longinus.

There was a look on the face of the saint that momentarily distracted Byron. It was enough for the raven to fly speedily past Byron, nearly hitting his face with his wings.

"Blast you, bird!!" Byron yelled, shaking his fist in the air.

He sighed in defeat and leaned his old bones up against the sturdy sarcophagus. "You win, Aidenn," he said out loud even though the bird was long gone. "You're not worth it, you troublemaker! I'm leaving now – and good luck finding your way back out of these old catacombs!"

In a brief moment of despair, he looked back at Saint Longinus. "I know what you're thinking," he told the statue, looking at its long face. "Good luck *myself* getting out of here. If the ghosts and haunts don't get me first, I'll be joining you after I starve to death. At least I am in good company."

The monk looked the statue up and down, recalling the saint's own sad story. "Forgive me. It is best I don't complain, when I compare this to your own tragedy. The centurion who pierced the side of Christ himself with a spear, causing a cascade of . . ."

A spear?

It couldn't be. The spear the Black Knight found earlier . . . was there a connection? Legends spoke of how Longinus the Centurion pierced the side of Jesus Christ himself as he hung upon the cross.

"But one of the soldiers with a spear pierced his side, and forthwith blood and water came out," Byron recited. "John 19:34."

He looked up at the saint. "And then the temple veil was torn in two, and the earth quaked, and the rocks were split. According to the Book of Matthew, the centurions who witnessed this said, 'Truly this was the Son of God'! You must have been one of those centurions, were you not, Saint Longinus?"

Wistfully the old monk wondered aloud, "To behold and know the Son of God in such a moment, whether centurion or citizen – such an event of the likes eclipsing all other events . . ."

Byron's eyes fell to the base of the statue in observance of something he didn't notice earlier – a suit of armor carved in stone sitting by the saint's right leg. It was a symbol of his past, representing a life of war behind him.

Surprisingly there wasn't a spear.

To his right the saint's future was displayed. A small table featured a Holy Bible, the robes of a priest, and a handheld cross, all of which were sculpted from the same stone material as the statue.

"The guilt you felt must have been unfathomable," he said, somberly. "I imagine that is why you cast aside your armor and took up the robes of a priest, carried your cross, and preached the Bible, ultimately becoming a saint."

The statue looked back at him, but didn't say a word.

Byron took a closer look, noticing the phenomenal detail behind the statue. Every chiseled line on his face, each curve of muscle, and every aspect on the stone objects were made up of exquisite detail and looked so incredibly lifelike, as if the real face of Longinus were frozen in time.

"Why was I brought before you, dear saint?" Byron asked, as though wondering if his presence were more than coincidence.

There was something on the ground near the base of the sculpted armor they hadn't noticed before, likely due to the dark shadows of the alcove. Byron pointed to a handful of stone pages. They were carved to illustrate a ragged edge where they seemed to have been torn out of the Bible on the table.

Byron took a closer look, pulling out his bifocals. There were actual words on the stone pages.

A dark shadow rushed out from behind the statue and sailed past him, seizing his heart with fear. Byron screamed, recklessly waving his torch and almost falling over.

The shadow was gone just as quickly as it surfaced, giving him doubts as to the authenticity of what his eyes claimed to see. Once his heart rate stabilized, convinced that whatever just happened was all in his imagination, he said, "It's almost as if these pages are evil."

It took a moment to gather himself and continue reading. That was the moment when he realized the significance of his discovery. "These are actual transcribed pages from the *Book of Death*!" he exclaimed.

Byron looked upwards, as if peering into the heavens. "Why must you torture me, Oh God?" It was a sobering, frightening thought to realize that the saint's name was quite possibly in the Book of the Dead – at least before he received salvation and picked up his cross to follow the Christ, thereby erasing his name and instead adding it to the Book of Life.

The spear, the pages – everything was slowly coming together. There was a reason why he stumbled into this place, and it had something to do with the Black Knight's quest.

Byron quickly pulled out a few blank parchments from his bag, along with a black piece of charcoal. Carefully he held a sheet down over one of the stone notes and scrubbed the charcoal sideways across the page until every individual letter and word was successfully transcribed. He did it again and again until he had copies of each and every one – now all he had to do was bring them, along with the new information about the spear, to the Black Knight.

There would be time to read and analyze the manuscripts along the way.

***

33 But when they came to Jesus and found that he was already dead, they did not break his legs. 34 Instead, one of the soldiers pierced Jesus' side with a spear, bringing a sudden flow of blood and water. 35 The man who saw it has given testimony, and his testimony is true. He knows that he tells the truth, and he testifies so that you also may believe. 36 These things happened so that the scripture would be fulfilled: "Not one of his bones will be broken," 37 and, as another scripture says, "They will look on the one they have pierced."

John 19:33-37

***

"I know it's here! I can feel it *calling* to me," an excited Emmeline told Elias, balancing her walk over the rubble of the destroyed castle between caution and her impulse to rush as fast as possible.

Elias followed her closely, nervously looking over both shoulders while simultaneously trying not to sprain an ankle with an ill-placed step.

It amazed him how she grew more confident and less afraid with each step. He was – like any normal human being – the exact opposite.

Even the crows, rats and snakes feared this place. There were no signs of life, and there hadn't been for the last several miles. An

131

occasional howl from a wolf in the far off distance was all they heard.

Something near the line of lifeless black trees drew his attention. Elias slowed down to take a better look. Each tree bore the same gnarled, sharp and pointy branches, seemingly reaching up in desperation to the night sky. They had thin, contorted limbs as though they had agonized in the flames of Hell. One of the dead trees stood out because it had a long vine hanging from it. No – not a vine. A rope. After closer inspection, Elias realized that it was a hangman's noose. *Why would there be a hangman's noose this close to a ruined, destroyed castle?*

"Keep *up!*" Emmeline scolded Elias with a paradoxically loud whisper. Her previous bratty behavior was acceptable, but she was becoming worse and he couldn't help but wonder if this place was having an effect on her.

He bounded over a few rectangular stones. "I'll keep up if you use a little more caution," he responded in a hushed tone, upset that she took his attention away from the tree.

Looking back to the same old, dead tree, Elias couldn't seem to find the hangman's noose. He strained his eyes and moved his head to change angles, but it was as if it was never there in the first place.

"Hey! Look over at those trees. Do you see anything strange?" He whispered to Emmeline.

Obsessed in her own endeavors, she either didn't hear him or ignored him. He sighed and wrote it off, trying to convince himself that the rope was never there in the first place.

"I wonder what it will feel like on my head. Do you suppose it will be heavy or light? I suspect something that grand and majestic should weigh a lot, but then again the finest craftsman in the land with the finest materials should guarantee it to be as light as a feather – that's the way a royal Queen would want it," she said.

Elias wondered if she was talking to him, or talking just to hear herself speak.

"They say the one who created the crown was actually a celestial being, maybe an angel. That would make sense for such a splendid, valuable piece of art. I've also heard . . ."

"Stop talking! You're going to wake the dead." Taking in his surroundings, he added, "And that's *not a good thing,* given we are standing on haunted grounds."

"Haunted," she sighed, slightly annoyed he interrupted her self-gratifying soliloquy. "Just be quiet and help me look for a way inside the castle."

"I hate to tell you, but every inch of the castle has been destroyed. There's not a way in. We really should be turning back; it's getting late."

"*LOOK!*" she exclaimed.

Emmeline hopped down off the rubble and to the ground. Placing her hands on her hips and flashing a cocky smile at Elias, her foot lightly tapped an old wooden trapdoor. "No way into the castle, huh? Not even despite the miles and miles of secret catacombs and passage ways deep below?"

Elias deflated. She was right, but he wasn't about to verbalize it. If her ego inflated any further, she'd float away.

Emmeline dropped to her knees and brushed the dust off old trapdoor. "No one will ever believe we found this! Come on, help me lift it up."

He hesitated at first, but reluctantly stepped forward.

She swung her head around, her eyes twinkling as she gazed into his. "Just imagine what might lie beneath! I bet we'll find not only the crown, but all sorts of other treasures. Ancient gold coins, jewelry and gems, even priceless artwork! Oh, how wonderful would that be? I'll be just like a princess!"

He was mildly surprised she actually directed her comments at him.

"I don't want to crush your spirit, but we don't even know if the tales are true."

"But they *are* true! I know it in my heart. I can't explain it. I can practically hear a royal anthem being played down below, just for me. I might actually become royalty!"

The trapdoor was heavier than it looked, but Elias managed to heave it open with her help. Its rusty hinges squeaked loudly as the heavy door flipped down to the ground, crashing loudly and sending up a cloud of dust and debris. The noise could've been heard for miles, waking up any slumbering creature – living or otherwise.

"CAREFUL, you fool!" she half whispered, half yelled.

She immediately followed up her curt behavior by flashing him a guilty look, blanching at her own behavior. She opened her mouth to apologize with genuine sincerity, but nothing came out.

Elias didn't seem to notice. He grabbed her by the arm and pulled her down, ducking behind a large concrete chunk of the fallen castle, hiding as if every watchful eye from across the hallowed grounds spotted them. They both held their breath and strained their ears, audibly searching for the sounds of a specter, or perhaps an apparition, floating up and over the rubble. Other than the cry of an owl far off in the distance – and the thumping of their own hearts – the night was dead.

Emmeline finally spoke, this time with a much more prudent whisper, "How much oil does your lantern have left?"

"Maybe three hours?" Creeping over to the open hole in the ground, he dared to look into the black void, dreading what might be lurking below. With wide eyes, he looked at her questioningly.

She scrunched her eyebrows and pointed resolutely at the hole.

Elias sighed and, with hands shaking, removed part of the lantern's hood just enough to direct the light down below.

Emmeline pulled a spool of purple thread out of her pocket and began tying one end to a loose chunk of rock.

Elias blinked. "Are we really sewing a shirt right now?"

"Laugh all you want. I brought this to make sure we don't get lost down there!"

She immediately grabbed the ladder rung and eagerly began climbing down into the deep, dark pit. "I can't see!" she gasped. "Come on!"

He shook his head with disbelief at what he was about to do. Despite a heavy fear weighing down his heart, he wasn't about to let her go alone. There wasn't any doubt she would've gone without him. With a slight tremble, he steadied himself on the ladder and followed her into the abyss.

The lantern's light flickered down the gloomy corridor, dancing upon the rough earthen walls. A nest of spiders scattered from the light of the lantern as it dared to encroach upon their territory, sending them deep into hidden cracks.

The more Elias found himself unnerved, Emmeline proved to be even more unwavering and steadfast in her personal expedition. She was a brave girl no doubt, but Elias was concerned her emboldened nature was – unnatural. Even the bravest of warriors had moments of fear and doubt.

"Keep the light steady," she whispered firmly. "I know we are getting closer!"

He tried to be gracious to the assertive girl, but his uneasiness made him question her. "How do you know? All we have seen are endless twisting caverns, and this exceptionally long passage that seems to lead to nowhere!"

I know, I know, he thought to himself before she could even answer. *Because it is calling to you.*

"I . . . just know, okay? Less talk, more help," she spat.

"You are obsessed. You know that, right?"

She completely ignored him; something else had her attention.

"Shut up! Look," she said, pointing her finger down the passage.

As Elias shone the light forward, illuminating the jagged tunnel walls, the cavern melded into a smooth, stone-worked hallway. Even the floor flattened out, covered by a long, red carpet stretching along the hallway and into the darkness.

There was something discomforting about the way the tunnel blended into a man-made passage, but they both cautiously followed along the red carpet.

"We are truly inside what's left of Wraithfall Castle," she said cryptically, "far below the ruins."

Paintings lined the entire length of the hallway, old portraits of men and women forgotten by time. An occasional small tabletop, statue bust, or suit of armor rested close to the wall, filling in empty spaces between the paintings.

It was hard to say how long the hallway was. On one hand it seemed to go on forever, but Elias knew his paranoia was only growing and it was quite possible that a few seconds felt like an hour, and an hour might pass in only a few seconds.

Emmeline gasped as the end of the hallway came into view. A lonely dais up against the far wall held a golden bust of an unknown female as if she were overseeing the entire corridor. Blackish-green stains ran underneath her eyes as if her tears tarnished her own golden skin, further decayed by the sands of time, but the sad tears were in stark contrast to the contorted disproportioned scowl and bitter coldness emanating from the woman.

A crown of pure solid gold sat atop her head – a real, honest to goodness crown of royalty. It seemed too large for the bust, but that only made it appear more extravagant.

Emmeline froze the moment she laid eyes on it, at first disbelieving what she saw, but that quickly passed. Before Elias could blink, the crown was in her hands. She twirled around and lifted up the crown, admiring it with wide eyes.

To say it was exquisitely crafted was an understatement. Detailed engravings etched into the crown told a story of a princess from beginning to end (from birth to death) until it met full circle and started all over again. The front of the crown initiated the mosaic with the newborn baby princess. Gradually as she grew older, her stages of life displayed on the crown blended into the next phase – after the baby princess came the little girl, and then a young teenager. Soon she became a young woman and married the man of her dreams, and then had a baby of her own. Finally they both grew older until they were elderly, and the story concluded with matching gravestones until the circle of life repeated at the very beginning – where another newborn baby princess was born.

At the top of the crown sat an angel sculpted from a large, pure diamond – the only jewel on the entire crown of gold – watching over the brand new baby girl throughout the entire span of her life.

Emmeline's fingertips carefully brushed over the diamond angel, admiring how it peacefully smiled down over the scene of life. "You were watching her the entire time, weren't you?" she whispered privately, but the angel did not reply.

"This is why they call you the Queen's Heaven."

Even Elias was shocked that they actually found the crown. "I was expecting it to be with the queen's body, but I guess the king would've had it taken from her before he buried her alive."

She gently placed the crown on her head, inhaling deeply and holding her breath as if she couldn't believe this moment existed. Emmeline squealed exuberantly, unable to contain her excitement.

"Isn't it *beautiful?* Especially the angel! I swear, I'm going to keep this and wear it until the day I die! Even when I bathe, even when I shower!" She quickly started looking around the hallway for a mirror so she could see her own reflection.

Elias grumbled, "If we don't get out of here soon, that day may come sooner than you think."

She turned up her nose at him. "Humph! You're no fun. Try as you may, I'm not going to let you steal my joy!"

Their conversation drifted into body language – and they both understood each other clearly.

He crossed his arms.

She rolled her eyes.

He didn't flinch – except for cocking his head to the side.

"Okay, *fine!* We can go . . . now that I have my crown. *Nobody* is going to believe our adventure!"

***

Act III, Scene 1

[The curtains open to a forlorn and desolate cemetery with a backdrop of dead black trees. A lone gravedigger stands up to his knees in a freshly dug grave. The moon hangs high. The only sound is the gravedigger's shovel scooping and tossing the dirt over his shoulder.]

Gravedigger: Late is the hour of the White Widow. *(Briefly looks up at the Moon.)* But then you knew that, didn't you? *(Resumes slow digging.)* Eternal night resides where she wanders, and you never drift too far away. Only by your generous light do we see, your light likened to a crumb of food thrown from the master's table for us dogs.

Moon: *(Slightly dims.)*

Gravedigger: Oh, I do not mean contempt, for we all are dogs – some rabid, some powerful, some starving. Some *dead.* Yes, were it not for the box given to the king by the gaunt and pale man, the White Widow would not haunt, nor would she *be.* And we would not be blessed with your glorious dim light. Her followers were so evil that when they tried to cast their sins into the box, thinking they could be free, there was nothing good left in them except a lifeless shell of flesh because . . . *(Chuckles)* they WERE sin – so *full* of sin. They turned to her for salvation but she couldn't save them."

Moon: *(Moonlight blinks twice, as if communicating.)*

Gravedigger: *(Chuckles)* I agree; most ironic. As if a box could save them. *She* couldn't save them, but she can *control* them – her evil and vile followers, now shadows at her beck and call. Oh but her powers over shadow – how she sniffs the life out of flesh and blood, only to turn muscle and bone into pure shadow, ever adding these horrors to her ever-growing army. It was as if she harnessed the powers of the Great Reaper itself.

(Cue the Scream in the background)

Gravedigger: *(Ducks down low in grave, looks up to the Moon)* she draws closer – closer yet and closer *still.* For now I must go and hide, oh Moon. Do not cast your light on me, lest she find me, my dear friend.

(Lowers himself into the grave, covers himself with dirt)

(Cue shadows elongating from the trees, converging on the grave where the Gravedigger lies)

- *Lost pages from* Confessional of Weeping Bones, *a forgotten play of centuries long past, author unknown.*

***

If it wasn't for the way the torchlight danced against the cavern wall, revealing a narrow vertical slit among the shadows – of which all of his instincts screamed out that it was a trap – Elias might've never managed to knock Emmeline out of the way just as a series of blades sprung out from the wall.

While Emmeline was safe, the blades nicked Elias just as he pushed her away. It could've been worse – had she sprung the trap a fraction of a second later he wouldn't have been able to jump clear of the razor-sharp blades, but he wasn't about to tell her and have her hysteria worsen.

"I'm so, *so sorry!*" Emmeline cried, pleading for forgiveness. Sniffing through her tears, she tried dabbing away at his wound with the edge of her dress before tearing off a strip of the fabric.

"For the tenth time, its okay," Elias told her, grunting in pain and wiping sweat off his brow as she pressed the blood-soaked cloth underneath his ribcage. His wounds from the blades weren't very deep, but he'd be lying if he said it wasn't painful.

This was no longer a game. They were long past the adventures of a simple treasure hunt or becoming a crowned princess – both of them nearly died.

To make matters worse, they were hopelessly lost.

After they found the crown, the two youth tried following the purple thread back to the ladder which led out of the cave, but beyond explanation the path laid out by the thread didn't lead to the ladder.

Defying all logic it took them in a circle. They were shocked to find themselves in the same dead-end hallway where they started.

The bust of the woman that once wore the crown was still at the end of the hall – or *was* it the same? The entire hallway looked identical, including the bust, except for one questionable detail: The original angry, hateful scowl on her face was now a scornful, contemptuous smile.

It wasn't until they fled from the hall a second time, frantically trying to find a way out, that they accidentally triggered the deadly trap.

***

Both sat in stunned silence for several minutes as Elias recovered.

"There *has* to be a way out," Emmeline said, breaking the silence.

"Not necessarily," he murmured ominously. "To say this place is haunted is an understatement. I'm not so sure there *is* a way out!"

"I....I want to go home," she whispered softly on the verge of tears – exacerbated by feelings of guilt and worry for his well-being, but predominantly out of an impending sense of hopelessness and doom.

He didn't fully understand why she felt that way – she was generally a pain, and he didn't think she was capable of misting up – but he nonetheless felt compelled to comfort her. He'd never seen this tender and exposed side of her. It was awkward, but he leaned forward to give her a hug. Before his arms were even up and open she leapt into his chest and began to sob hysterically.

His eyes grew wide and he wasn't sure what to do, but he gradually allowed his arms to close around her and allow her cry. His body, cold from the chilly night air, gained a comfortable warmth from her body heat. There wasn't any question that she embraced him because she was afraid, but his heart beat furiously anyway.

He was about to dismiss his irregular heartbeat as nothing more than a fear at their hopeless situation – and legitimately so – when she leaned back and looked at him with damp eyes. There was something about the way she stared at him that captivated him. Contradicting the cold unfriendliness he was used to from Emmeline, there was a warm gentleness reflected that he hadn't seen before.

Her eyes locked on his. He was nervous and uncertain of what to do. He wanted to look away, but he didn't want to be a coward. She was looking to him for support.

Do something. Anything, he told himself. But what – he didn't have a clue.

Elias started humming a familiar song, one that he remembered his mother singing to him before she passed away. He wasn't sure why he chose now of all moments. He usually hummed to himself at the orphanage whenever he was nervous or uncomfortable – maybe that was why. With his side split open, that seemed like a pretty good excuse.

Emmeline glanced at him with unique curiosity, followed by a gentle smile rising upon her face.

Before he knew it, Elias found his body gently swaying to his own humming. His side-to-side motion became more pronounced. He was humming a song to a girl that ridiculed him not even hours before, and within moments she was laughing in spite of her tear-stained cheeks.

It was impossible to forget they were trapped below ground, but both of their fears were dampened. They found themselves both on their feet, moving to the rhythm of his song while slow dancing in the darkness. Once she took note of the melody, she joined him in a soft, meek hum, following his lead.

Even though Emmeline wasn't with her boyfriend, she didn't seem to be missing the dance back at the orphanage after all. By the look on her face, the laughter in her voice and the twinkle in her eye, he was pretty sure she was okay with it.

Elias accidentally stepped on her foot and stammered out an apology, but she giggled quietly and told him not to worry about it.

He resumed the dance the best he could, and even when he stopped humming it was still as if the music was playing in the background. He moved his head in closer, and she responded as if pulled in by his movement. Their lips were inches apart. He breathed harder, and judging by the warmth of her breath he was fairly certain her breathing also grew more rapid. Her eyelids gently closed, and she waited.

Aware that the self-made music was gone, replaced by an eerie silence in the air, he panicked. His confidence waned and, instead of kissing her – as badly as he wanted to – he drew her in for a hug.

Elias sighed to himself and swallowed hard, knowing he messed up. After a short delay, Emmeline hugged him back. At least he wasn't *totally* humiliated.

When he dared to pull away Elias, unable to hide the guilty look on his face, was at least relieved to see her smile was still there.

***

"...Who forsakes the companion of her youth, And forgets the covenant of her God.

18 For her house leads down to death, And her paths to the dead;

19 None who go to her return, Nor do they regain the paths of life"

Proverbs 2:17-19

***

Clamping his old knobby knees against the aged mule and hunkering his bony frame downwards, Byron the Wise carefully swung a leg behind him and dismounted the burdened beast, using his old oaken walking staff for support.

"Keep your eyes open," he whispered to the raven and the mule.

The burning sensation on the inside of his leg nearly caused it to buckle under his weight, as light as he may have been – only his trusty staff saved him from falling to the ground. It made him once again question why he was out here.

Even tying off the mule to an old knobby tree proved a challenge as the edgy, uncooperative animal resisted, wanting nothing more than to turn back and leave.

"I don't want to be here anymore than you, you stubborn creature," he scolded it.

If there was a bright spot, it was that there was plenty of old, dead wood devoid of moisture on the ground – easy to gather, easy to light. Byron had a campfire going in no time.

"Heh . . . not bad, if I do say so myself," he panted, dusting off his hands and sitting on a nearby log, soaking in the warmth from the flames.

"Now let's see," he said, adjusting the thin frame of his glasses and pulling out the charcoal rubbings. The moment his fingers touched the paper, a cold chill ran through his body.

Aidenn immediately let out a squawk and took to the air, abandoning the old man.

"Bah! Some help you are."

Even though it was nothing more than a silly bird, the dwelling fear of the old man slightly amplified with the departure of his traveling companion.

It took him a few moments to take a deep breath and settle his old heart.

He cleared his throat and coughed on his fist.

Byron slowly raised the pages to take a better look by the fire's light, his hand trembling from the tremors of the elderly, but also augmented by trepidation.

For an unexplained reason, the mule began to bray and pull against the rope binding him to the tree. "Quiet, beast! Are you *trying* to wake the dead? Now hush!" he scolded it. The mule settled down only slightly, but enough for Byron to try to return to his charcoal rubbings.

Before he could read the pages something caught his eye. There was an imposing individual sitting next to the fire opposite where he sat – Byron nearly jumped three feet high at this discovery. He gasped and lowered his notes, clutching his hand at his heart. No living creature would be this far into the forest – did the Black Knight sneak up on him again?

"I say, dear knight, you mustn't do that! How did you know I would be here? I expected you further along and near the ruins."

After receiving no response, Byron peered his head around the fire to get a better look.

Whoever it was wore an old and tattered white cloak. White – most certainly *not* what a knight of black would wear. His heart thumped faster.

"W-who . . . who are you?! Do speak up!"

His request was met with grave silence.

Byron tucked his notes away and grasped the staff quietly resting against the log. Carefully – and regretfully – he worked his way around the fire.

Suddenly there was a loud *pop* from the fire, dwarfing all earlier crackling sounds, so loud it startled Byron and nearly caused him to drop his staff.

The mule was spooked so badly it started braying and tugging again, but with ten times the intensity. The rope snapped, and before Byron could get a word out, the animal bolted off into the night, swallowed up by the darkness and abandoning his master.

The old man white-knuckled his staff with two hands, pointing one end defiantly at the unknown trespasser. As he took another step closer, the wind shifted direction, fanning the flames of the fire and causing the smoke to drift between the two of them before rising into the night.

"*Answer me*! Identify yourself!"

The white-shrouded individual turned their cloaked head toward Byron.

And there, to his horror, the old man saw by the fire's light nothing more than a *hollow darkness* underneath the white hood.

An empty face. A *headless* apparition.

Byron screamed in terror and fell backwards, dropping his staff. A sudden pain surged inside his chest, causing his entire body to tense up.

He tried to scramble away, desperately attempting to stand on his own two feet, noticing the tattered white cloak flapping in the wind's gentle breeze as he looked over his shoulder.

The old man scuttled and scampered, uncertain of how much distance he gained, but the pain in his chest wouldn't let him run any longer. He collapsed to the forest floor, face down in the dirt.

What was that thing? Was it following him? Was it nothing more than a torn cloak caught in the branches, swayed by the lightly blowing gusts?

Was all of this simply a misapprehension all along? He could have *sworn* he saw it actually turning to face him.

Byron winced as the pain surging throughout his body grew in intensity. His old shaking hand reached deep into his oversized pockets and pulled out all of the notes and his piece of charcoal. "Aidenn! *Aiiiiiidenn!*" he screamed breathlessly, trying to summon the raven.

He looked over his shoulder again – if that horror was chasing him, there wasn't much time before his impending doom.

A feather and ink would have been more appropriate, but time wasn't on his side. Byron flipped one of the papers over and wrote on the back of it with the charcoal, trying to steady his hand as much as possible.

Just as he started rolling and binding the papers up with a piece of twine, Aidenn landed by his side.

His breathing was growing weaker. Pushing the rolled-up papers to the raven, he wheezed, "The Black Knight . . . he *must* s-see these. H-he . . . he . . ."

Obeying his master, the raven grabbed the string in its talons and flew off, blending in with the dark skies.

Byron would've sighed with relief if he didn't feel his very soul slipping away from his body. He clutched his heart and rolled over on his side, wondering which would happen first – his body giving out, or the white-cloaked undead creature claiming him.

"Take me, Christ, before it finds me. Do not let it . . . *turn* me. Your will be done."

He heard movement in the forest approaching him before breathing his last.

***

"During those days people will seek death but will not find it; they will long to die, but death will elude them."
Revelations 9:6

***

It was said that time was a mischievous creature, and never was that more true than underneath the castle's ruins where day and night did not exist. In spite of that, Elias and Emmeline were certain of two things.

First, they had been down there for *way too long*, regardless of whether or not the sun's presence graced the earth above.

Secondly, they were still lost.

"I know you don't want to hear this, but the oil is running low," Elias told Emmeline, hinting that the lantern's fuel would soon run dry and plunge them into utter darkness.

To his surprise, she didn't seem concerned. Then again she could've been ignoring him. Being underground for so long was doing funny things to his mind. It wasn't uncommon to see things that weren't really there, or shadows slithering just outside his field of vision. Going left and right didn't seem to make any difference – it was almost as if the underground corridors were leading them where *it* wanted to.

"I thought as much," a dejected Emmeline responded. Dark rings circled her tired eyes. She was still quite beautiful regardless, but Elias could tell her morale was waning.

"Hey, can I ask you something," Elias asked her, thinking of conversational topics. He found the more they talked about normal life outside of the ruins, the more likely it was for her to forget about their abysmal situation, even if only temporary.

She shrugged, "Why not? Now is as good of a time as any."

"Why do you insist on being called 'Lady Emmeline'? We both know that isn't your real name."

She smiled, adjusting her crown. It was as if the mere touch of her fingertips to its gold surface reminded her of her royal importance – even if she wasn't *really* royalty.

"Because. I just like it."

"That's not an answer," Elias countered. "Besides, I kind of like the name . . ."

"Don't *say* it! I don't like my name."

"But it's what makes you who you are."

"No it doesn't. Who you are on the *inside* is what makes you who you are. A name is just a label."

But if it was just a label, then again – why didn't she like it?

"So . . ."

She ignored him. After a few moments passed without any reply, he added, "It's not like you don't have time to tell me."

She huffed and pouted, "Fine."

Emmeline took a few moments to compose her thoughts before answering him.

"I can't *stand* my name. Okay? The few memories I do have of my father weren't good ones."

He whispered quietly and with the slightest awe, "You remember your father?"

She scoffed and rolled her eyes. "Sadly, yes. Every time I heard him call my name – or rather, *yell* my name in a drunken rage, I . . . remember a feeling of sickness in the pit of my stomach. Everything that would happen next was . . ."

Emmeline swallowed hard. Her voice turned cold. "Tell me. Have you *ever* heard of a princess abused by the hand of her father, the king? Have you ever heard of a princess living *unhappily* ever after?"

Elias grew quiet.

Maybe he underestimated her. She always appeared spoiled. High and mighty. Snarky, mean, and greater than everybody else. He was starting to understand why she was molded and shaped that way.

"I . . . I'm sorry he hurt you. I don't remember my parents."

"That's a *good* thing," she snapped.

Her shoulders sank and her mood suddenly changed. "I'm so sorry. I didn't mean that."

"That's okay. I can understand why you feel that way. Isn't it ironic? I would give anything to have the slightest *glimpse* of a memory of my mother and father, and I believe you would do anything to erase yours."

She sniffed, "I'm sorry, Elias. This is all my fault."

"You mustn't blame yourself."

"But it is! If . . . if we die here, who will remember two little orphans? *No one,* that's who!"

Elias took a deep breath and put a hand on her shoulder.

"Every orphan in our house will remember you, Emmeline. You're unforgettable," he laughed, causing her to chuckle.

"That doesn't sound like a compliment."

"Perhaps part of it wasn't, but resoundingly the other part *was* a compliment. You will be remembered. And even if you were not, well . . . even if we both were not to make it out alive, you can be sure wherever we go next, what waits us on the other side, *I* will know and remember you."

Those words alone made her smile and brought her a sense of peace – even if only for a short while.

"You just called me *Emmeline,*" she said, flashing a teasing smile.

He rolled his eyes. "No I didn't."

Wait . . . he did, didn't he?

His words of denial didn't matter – she *knew,* and was bound to never let him forget.

He pursed his lips. "Let's just keep moving."

It wasn't long before they stood yet again at another junction. The pathways carried on for only a short while, both ending in darkness.

"I don't know which way to go," he said despondently.

She didn't say anything – it was as if she were stuck in her own little world.

"Are you okay? Which way do you think we should go? Left or . . ."

The girl stepped past him and cut him off as if she didn't even notice him speaking. "Do you hear that? That beautiful melody . . . it's coming down the hall!"

She turned the corner cautiously and advanced with one foot in front of the other.

Elias shined the lantern ahead of her. "I . . . don't hear anything," he said, straining his ears. "Are you sure?"

"Yes! It's down the hallway," she exclaimed excitedly. Her once-hesitant steps quickly turned into a brisk walk.

Her carelessness stunned him. "Wait! Don't forget about the traps! Don't . . ."

His words were futile as she held the crown on her head and ran forward out of the lantern's range, vanishing into the darkness.

"Are you crazy?" He scampered after her, wondering what was getting into her.

"*The music*! I've never heard a song like this before! *It's beautiful!* Almost like an angelic chorus."

He couldn't hear a thing other than his heartbeat pounding in his ears and the oxygen inhaled through his throat. "I don't hear a thing!"

By the time he caught up to her, he noticed a deep dark pit only a few steps ahead of her. Apparently her obsession was blinding her because she didn't seem to notice. Before Elias could so much as grunt a warning to her, he lunged forward and grabbed her arm.

"What are you . . ." she started to say as he tugged her back, but her words fell short as her foot slipped off the ledge.

Elias dropped his lantern and grabbed her with both hands, leaning backward to prevent them both from falling in.

Her crown slipped off of her head and she screamed, but she succeeded in grabbing it before it plunged down the seemingly bottomless shaft.

The lantern shattered and oil spilled across the ground. The small flickering flame somehow managed to avoid the oil, instead vanishing and allowing the darkness to engulf them.

Elias couldn't believe she would risk her life for that *stupid* crown – let alone nearly take him down the hole with her. But for now, they were both safe.

Emmeline finally realized how close she came to falling down the dark shaft. She squeezed Elias, wrapping her arms tightly around him. "T-thank you," she whispered fearfully.

He took a deep breath and asked her, "Are you okay? This . . . you've been acting – *strange*."

"Yes, I'm fine," she quickly answered while standing and fixing her dress, trying to compose herself.

"We are completely blind," Elias said. "All we can do is follow the wall and try to avoid any more pitfalls. We need to find a source of light as soon as . . ."

"Look over there! There is light up ahead! That must be where the music is coming from."

"Forget about the music!"

"Well, right now this path takes us to our only source of light, like it or not. Let's just see what's up ahead."

Elias still didn't hear the music, but as his eyes adjusted to the darkness, he did catch a very feint trace of light further down the tunnel. She was right – with the broken lantern at their feet, what other choice did they have?

"Hold on to the wall as you walk around the edge of the pit. We don't need you falling in it again."

He expected her to brush him off, but to his surprise she gave him a soft, "Okay."

After they skirted around the edge of the pit on a narrow ledge, blindly tapping with one foot at a time to avoid any missteps, they both found it was a short walk to the source of light – its illumination slightly increased with each step, becoming larger as the tunnel widened.

The corridor emptied out into a small, dimly lit chamber. Four lit torches rested in ornamental sconces, providing the faint illumination that Emmeline noticed.

"Somebody must have been here recently," Elias said, nodding towards the torches that could only have been lit by human hands. "Or maybe they still are."

A plain stone table devoid of any adornments – possibly an altar – sat covered in cobwebs in the center of the room. There was a single object sitting on the table, black in color and difficult to make out given the way it blended in with the shadows.

"You're right! And the music box is playing," she said without turning around to look at him, she was so deeply focused on the decorative box on the center of the table. It was almost as if she were in a daydream. "The song is *so beautiful*!"

"Music? What are you talking about? Emmeline, we shouldn't be here. Something about this feels . . . wrong. It's like there's evil in the very air that surrounds us – or rather *engulfs* us," Elias said, looking over both shoulders.

"Something is watching us . . . I can *feel* it. We need to go."

His ears picked up a strange sound – there *was* music. She was right! As Elias strained to hear the far off noise, he realized something horrific. It wasn't a joyous music box that he heard. It was more like a hissing sound – the string of a lone violin. But it sounded . . . evil. Demonic. Far away, but approaching rapidly.

A cold shiver ran down his spine, and he grew terrified.

Emmeline approached the altar, so transfixed with the object she either didn't hear Elias or was ignoring him altogether – either way, she didn't respond.

Elias strained his voice, quietly yelling, "What are you . . . *don't* touch that!"

His instincts told him to run, but he couldn't leave her. The shriek of the violin grew louder. "Wait – the music is coming from that . . . thing. Whatever it is, it's not a music box. That shape . . ."

Emmeline didn't blink, and she didn't hesitate. The object of desire reflected in her eyes from the flickering of the dimly lit torches. "It's beautiful," she whispered, as if in a trance.

She reached for the lid.

"No! *Don't*!" he tried to warn her.

She didn't listen.

He lurched at her, grabbing her shoulder and trying to pull her away, but it was too late.

Emmeline took the lid off the urn.

Not a music box – a black, concave-shaped *urn*.

Wide-eyed and panicked, he yelled out of fright, loud enough for his voice to carry the entire length of the tunnel, and called her by her real name – *"Pandora, STOP!"*

Wisps of black leaked out of the box-like urn, flooding the room with shadows. From within the urn, the low hissing sound of the violin grew into numerous eerie sounds, each with a different pitch. Strands of blackness drowned out the torchlight. Some of the shadows slithered while others seemed to float, defying the very air it traversed.

Suddenly the blackness rushed down the hall like a swarm of bats tasting the freedom of the night's air.

The force and power coming from the urn knocked her off balance, causing the crown to fall from her head, tumble to the ground and roll until it settled into a tight spinning circle, finally sitting motionless.

The white diamond angel on top of the crown known as Queen's Heaven had left – vanished into thin air as if it were never there.

The angel, once watching over the golden girl on the crown – *was gone.*

And a voice of terrible, tremendous evil shouted:

Come Forth.

Cursed is the left of the house.

Cursed is the right of the house.

Death is upon you.

Come Forth.

The hateful words penetrated the very marrow of his bones. It was impossible to tell if the evil speech came from the darkness, the hollow urn, or if it even originated inside his head – but it repeated over and over, reverberating within his skull.

Elias heard a blood-curdling scream from Pandora, but he couldn't locate her – it was impossible to see her through the pitch black or pinpoint her whereabouts with his ears as the sound echoed off the walls. Overwhelming fear and confusion drove him down the tunnel from where they came.

Death is upon you.

It echoed again and again. Before he knew it, his foot slipped and he lost his balance, nearly falling into the same pit he had just saved Pandora from. A cold gust – not of wind, but of something more unnatural – hit him square in the chest, rushing through his body as if he were hollow. It was as if the very cold itself grew claws of ice and shadow, ripping into his chest and burning his soul.

Elias opened his jaw and tried to scream, but nothing came out of his mouth as he fell backward into the deep black pit.

***

"For what is a shadow? A shadow always hides from the light. Its very nature is to slither and crawl, knowing the light will expose it for what it really is. When the light turns the corner, the shadow moves away, for it cannot stand the light . . ."
The Lost Book of Second Ephesians 11:13

***

It was a great debate among townsfolk how Wraithfall Castle *really* fell.

While many claimed an earthquake of godly proportions rocked the enormous castle to its very foundation, other rumors persisted in whispers that the rubble he stood on was a result of a great and sinister evil.

What Lies Beneath Wraithfall Ruins

Regardless of the truth, the fact remained that over half the castle plummeted hundreds of feet into the ocean below while the remainder of stonework simply collapsed upon itself, and the once magnificent architectural structure was no more.

There was an underground labyrinth within these ruins – ancient crypts and secret passages – some of which likely survived the castle's collapse. Steadfastly on guard with his sword drawn and shield at the ready, the knight navigated on top of, across, over and even under acres of rubble in order to find a way underground.

After reaching what could only be described as an apex of mountainous stone debris, he took notice of what appeared to at one time be a ballroom, now sunken into the earth on the other side of the wreckage. It was hard to say if the ballroom was originally underground, or if it was above ground before the earthquake and somehow survived the collapse as it came to rest an estimated ten to twenty feet below ground level.

Black and purple tile with spider-webbed cracks alternated in a checkered pattern, once covered by a detailed mural. Parts of the mural could be seen on the floor below, now open to the dark sky. Broken pillars painted with angels battling demons lay broken upon the floor.

Furniture, no longer recognizable, was little more than splintered debris. Evidence of several musical instruments, likely of considerable value once long ago, had also fallen victim to the castle's demise.

Even though the ballroom itself was in wretched condition, it was remarkable that even a small part of it had survived the cataclysmic event and remained relatively flat.

The knight spotted an opening beneath the rubble on the far side of the ballroom floor, apparently at one time a connecting hallway.

If the tunnel wasn't fully collapsed, there was a chance it might lead to the underground labyrinth below the former castle.

The knight carefully climbed down into the open ballroom. The moment his foot hit the floor, a quiet noise rose in the air, shaping itself into a familiar sound and rhythm. Though partially distorted, it was quite possibly only in his head.

A haunting melody.

He could almost envision the tune at a dance underneath a bright chandelier with jubilant laughter in the background, but the way the violins obsessed over bass notes and the harpsichord trilled somber, discordant notes, it came across more like a miserable, desolate dirge at a pauper's funeral. The octave and rhythm were clearly a distorted version of the original, as if a dark evil force had corrupted what was once cheerful and bright.

Pressed against the shadows of the night, figments within the corner of his eye fluttered and floated, as if dancing up in the air, where the ballroom floor *used* to be. They vanished when he turned his head to catch the shadows in the act, only to notice movement coming from the new realm of his peripheral.

Regardless of his visions, his instincts told him he wasn't alone.

A flash of black rapidly descended down on him, prompting him to take up an offensive stance with his sword. His arm was drawn back, fully ready to strike, when he noticed (at the last minute) it was the black raven.

He relaxed the grip on his weapon as the large bird landed on his shoulder, bearing loosely rolled papers tied off by a thin strand of thread.

"Aidenn. How did you find me?" he asked, while taking the papers from his beak. He wasn't expecting an answer, but the gripping insanity spread by Wraithfall Ruins reminded the warrior that nothing was certain.

The raven let out a caw.

It is coming.

The Black Knight froze at those words. He *swore* he heard the raven speak, but he refused to believe it. Of course the larger issue at hand was the three spoken – or rather *squawked* – words of warning.

It.

Is.

Coming.

A dark shadow originated from behind him, falling across the entire scape of the ruins.

The knight was almost out of time.

He grabbed the scrolls, tucking them away, and waved the raven away as he rushed across the ballroom, entering the tunnel.

***

The Black Knight continued running long after he grew weary – no threat of a collapsing ceiling, arduous jump across a pit of black, or questionable turn around a dark corner within the underground maze slowed him down.

Death was behind him.

He had evaded it for so long, but deep down he knew it would soon be over – he was on borrowed time and the bell would soon toll for his soul. If evil would strike him down, it didn't matter – he would still go and be with God. But it was of the utmost importance to complete his mission before that could happen.

Dark swirling masses gathered down the long corridor. He could see it – he could *feel* it. The Black Knight knew he was getting close.

He didn't stop and he didn't rest, and his persistence finally paid off – he knew exactly where he was.

The growing darkness chilled him to the bone, but he marched the long walk, chanting quietly under his breath, *Christus, salvum me fac*, repeating those words over and over. The further he marched, the stronger his conviction grew, his faith emboldening him despite this place of great evil.

The shadows were so overwhelming his vision gradually became obscured, eventually plummeting him in darkness. He felt against the walls, traveling down the tunnel carefully, until he felt the jagged texture of rock turn into a smooth man-made design.

It had to be here somewhere.

Despite the confusion within his mind, the Black Knight knelt down and felt around the floor. It seemed like an eternity, but he finally found what he was searching for – both the black urn and its lid.

As quickly as he could, he placed the lid on the urn, fighting against a great resistance as if a strong pressure were built up inside – as if the urn did not *want* the lid – but with every muscle in his body flexed and bearing a will of steel, he finally forced it on. He held it tightly in place as if subconsciously worried about possible leaks until he gave the lid a slight twist, locking it in place. Carefully he set it on the altar.

A great hiss went up in the air, and many of the shadows parted, revealing a small trace of light from dancing torches in the room. Much of the evil within was set free long ago, but with the urn now contained the knight somehow knew he was on the path to restoring what once was broken.

"Elias?"

The Black Knight quickly spun around. He hadn't heard that name in years. There was only one person that might possibly remember.

Emmeline – *Pandora* – stood before him. He never thought he would see her again.

After all of these years she was still beautiful, but she was also tragic. Her outfit was torn and tattered, her hair was knotted and unkempt, and her eyes were devoid of life. Her left hand still clutched the golden crown, grasping it so tightly that blood trickled down her hand.

How she was still alive was a mystery.

It finally sunk in that she was *real,* not merely a figment of his imagination. Elias ran up to her, but to his surprise she was jerked back into the darkness before he could reach her. Thin white strands like those from a predatory spider were attached to her like deathly white puppet strings, an unseen evil manipulating her movements.

"*No!*" he shouted, desperately lurching for her.

Rushing deep into the heart of darkness, he prayed and prayed – the only way he could keep the evil and insanity at bay.

He caught sight of Pandora once more – she was still being whisked down the hall, prompting him to push forward harder. Just beyond her he caught a glimpse of spectral white. He knew the haunt was her manipulator. He couldn't make out any distinguishable features of the ghoulish form except for what should've been its head – ghostly bandages were wrapped over its face as if wearing a death cocoon, and many of those bandages floated in the air as if it were submerged underneath gentle waves, blending in with its mist-like form.

After twist and turn down the winding passageways, he finally saw hope – a dead-end. They were cornered.

It wasn't merely where the caverns reached its end – the far wall was a deeper red shade compared to the rest of the natural grey cavern. It was smooth and man-made, built of brick and mortar.

He expected the white apparition to slow down but surprisingly it continued – *straight through the wall!*

And it took Pandora with her.

This isn't possible, he growled. Raising his shield, he charged into the wall, planning to smash it down with brute strength if necessary.

But it wasn't there. There was *never* a wall, evident by the way he continued straight through, stumbling over his own feet and falling to the ground.

Was this an evil illusion? Was this another mind-inducing effect from the spreading insanity – was he really going mad?

He looked around his surroundings on the other side of the *wall*. The cramped chamber showed evidence of pickaxe marks, revealing it was at one time long ago hastily dug and formed out of the natural cavernous foundation. Several alcoves were blocked off with iron bars, leading him to deduce that this was at one time a prison deep underneath the castle.

One of the far walls was excavated long ago to create a narrow tunnel of roughly fifty feet in length – partially preserved bodies hung from shackles spanning the entire distance, marking the location of their final moments. Judging by their decaying dresses they were all female, and each had a white bag covering their heads.

One of the bodies halfway down the tunnel moved – or rather twitched. The Black Knight could only assume a rat or scavenger was looking to feast.

It wasn't until Pandora ran up to hug him that he realized she was in the room.

Whatever was controlling her released her – *for now* – but there was still a heavy sense of lingering evil in the chamber. They were being watched.

His arms wrapped tightly around Pandora and he exhaled, "I'm sorry it took so long."

"Where am I, Elias? How long have . . . "

"You mean you don't remember what happened after that fateful night?"

She shook her head and cast her eyes downward out of guilt, clearly remembering her role in unleashing a great evil – but nothing after that.

He ran the fingers of his iron gauntlet across her back and arms carefully, feeling for any strings but unable to find an explanation for what just happened.

Knowing what he was searching for, her voice quaked as she told him, "I can't explain it either."

"What happened to you?"

She shrugged with uncertainty, genuinely unable to remember, but Elias wondered if her own fears weren't helping to block out her traumatization.

"We must go," he said. He grabbed her by the hand and turned around, expecting to exit through the illusion the same way they came in, but found that to his great surprise *it was now solid.*

They were trapped.

Both Elias and Pandora were disheartened, but Elias for a much greater reason.

"Emmeline, there is something you should know," he said cryptically. He turned around to face her, conveying the importance of his message.

"What is it?"

"Know that I will try to get us out of here – I will tear down that wall brick by brick if I have to. However . . ."

"Just say it, Elias," she spat out nervously, but with a twinge of resolve.

"I do not have much time left. Death is coming for me."

She furrowed her eyebrows, not understanding.

"Death himself – the Grim Reaper."

She gasped. "Does that have something to do with the evil that I….that I…."

He calmly placed a hand on her shoulder, forbidding her from finishing her incriminating sentence. He reminded her, "That wasn't your fault – maybe *partially*, but neither of us could stand against the great evil within this realm. There was a great influence upon you. Our mistake was entering this realm of evil, toying with forces beyond our power."

The knight continued, "That night, when I fell into the pit, Death tried to snatch me in its claws. I can feel the cold sting to this day – he left marks on my chest. On my soul, for which I am forever tainted until the second coming.

"But something happened when the Reaper reached out for me with its bony claws. As I fell into the pit, it . . . well, it partially *missed.* It was as if an Angel of God protected me from its soul-stealing grasp. However – I did not get away unscathed."

Pandora bit her lip, afraid of what he might say next.

"It grasped my shadow and tore it from my body. *I have no shadow.*"

As if unable to trust his very words – even though she believed him – she looked at one of the burning torches along the wall out of instinct, and then back to Elias, expecting to see his shadow anyway. She then looked at the ground behind her.

Pandora had a shadow.

He did not.

"Death comes for me, but not you. I swear to you, I will get you out of here," he proclaimed. Before she could respond, Elias turned to the wall and began to strike at it downward with the downward point of his shield.

"This is all my fault. Please, Elias – remove your helm so I can see you once again."

He smiled underneath his helm as he continued relentlessly striking at the wall, adding alternating blows with the hilt of his sword. "If we survive, I will gladly take off my helm for you, but for now there is no time to waste."

Before either knew what was happening, the brick wall disintegrated before their very eyes – Elias jumped back, instinctively placing himself in front of Pandora.

He knew why – it was time.

"It is here."

Despite the darkness of the long corridor, Elias could see, feel, even *smell* Death approaching.

For years Elias managed to hide from Death. Every time Death drew close to him, Elias found a way to escape. He once rode a horse as far to the west as possible, delaying the setting of the sun and prolonging the Reaper from arriving on the waves of night, putting further distance between. When that horse rode to exhaustion, he found another one and repeated the cycle.

This time there was nowhere to run or hide. The familiar smell of decay wafting down the stifling hall coincided with the black creature who remained deathly still except for a slight breeze daring to touch the base of its tattered black robe.

It was too late to save Pandora. She would die with him.

"*I can't move!*" Pandora screamed.

He turned around, witnessing scores of white string twisting around her and sticking to her body, keeping her frozen in place. It wouldn't take long until she was fully wrapped up inside the cocoon.

Elias had the feeling that instead of a spider coming to feast on her, she was being turned into a sacrifice.

"This is my fault! I never should've come here," she lamented. "I was selfish, greedy, and all of the evil I am responsible for . . . but most of all I led *you* here! Please forgive me, even though I'll never forgive myself for what I did to you!"

Elias wildly swung his sword at her binding strings, but with each batch that he severed, twice as many appeared from nowhere, further restraining her. Try as he might he couldn't keep up, and it would be a matter of time before he depleted all of his energy. "I made my own choices – that wasn't your fault."

"Leave me," she shouted as tears trickled down her face. "Save yourself, Elias! *Run!*"

"I'm not leaving you!" he shouted at her, refusing to give up.

As Death slowly closed in on them, floating slowly down the tunnel as if time were a matter foreign to it, Elias grew desperate. He knew his actions were futile, but he wouldn't go down without a fight.

Turning to face Death, Elias gripped his sword tightly and pulled out the broken spear, preparing to use every instrument available for their defense.

"Christ grant me strength," he growled in a prayer of equal passion, courage, and defiance up until the end.

"Listen to me, Death! I have avoided you for a long time, and now you have me. My soul is prepared to see the Christ – you may slay me, but even *you* cannot take my soul to Hades. But I ask you to spare Pandora, for this is not her time. I know that with enough time, she will come to know the Christ as well. *It is not her time.*"

Whether or not the Reaper understood, it did not respond and it did not show hesitation. It merely crawled forward at a slow, debilitating pace.

Pandora was helpless to physically assist, but her sharp eyes noticed something he did not. "Elias! Something fell out of your pouch when you pulled out your spear."

The once rolled-up papers of Byron the Wise slipped out of the string and now lay loose on the floor. One of the upside-down papers had a single handwritten word written on it: *LONGINUS.*

The word was enough to momentarily distract him from the encroaching threat. His brows furrowed as he focused on the word – and then, with wide-open eyes, he profoundly realized what he held in his hand. The spear of Saint Longinus.

Pandora shouted, "What are you doing?" as he dropped his large animal skin pack, pulled out a large leather-bound book and set it on the ground. He quickly flipped through the pages until he was where he wanted to be and read the words on the page.

"I see now," he whispered.

The Black Knight stood up and reached toward Pandora, tenderly wiping away a few tears from her eyes.

He took the wet fingertip of his gauntlet and gently rubbed it on the tip of the spear, dampening the long-dried blood.

The knight now had the blood of Jesus Himself on his fingertip. Bending over the Book of Death, he took his finger and brushed the blood across one of the many names in the book. *Her* name. Pandora Seraphia.

"By his stripes we are healed," he whispered.

As the black ink vanished, leaving a gap among the column of names, Pandora spasmed as a jolt coursed through her body. Just as quickly as the searing tremor from within her chest surged, it disappeared altogether.

The strings were now gone and she fell to her knees in shock. Blood rushed back though her body – she stared at her hands in amazement as her fingertips transformed from a ghostly pale white to warm, peach-colored flesh.

She heard a hiss from behind her, but she didn't turn around quickly enough to witness the white formless haze drift away from her presence and evaporate into thin air.

"Through the blood of Christ, it seems we didn't fail after all," the knight said, bending down to hug Pandora, allowing himself a small moment of victory.

Now that her name was stripped from the Book of Death, she had a chance at life. True, genuine life – freedom by the blood of Christ, both literally and symbolically. Despite her act of unleashing a horrendous evil, she was forgiven.

The look in her eyes said everything. She couldn't believe it – she felt alive again. All darkness within her – all blackness and every stain – felt as if it were stripped away

Pandora squeezed him as hard as she could, wrapping her arms around his black shell of armor. She almost took off his helmet to kiss him – until she noticed something down the hall.

The moment the knight saw her eyes shift from rapturous joy to grave horror he knew that, unlike the white apparition that vanished and no longer tormented her – Death was still coming.

***

"I looked, and there before me was a pale horse! Its rider was named Death, and Hades was following close behind him..."
Revelation 6:8

***

She would finally be safe, but his time was up.

"No! You can't do this," Pandora shouted, trying to step in between Elias and the dark soul-stealer, but Elias held out an arm and wouldn't let her pass.

Death was now before him, remaining at a hover, so close that it could touch Elias with its scythe if it so chose.

"And so I shall meet my maker," Elias whispered. "*'O Death, where is your sting? O Hades, where is your victory?'*"

Pandora fell to the floor, inconsolably sobbing. Elias, knowing she would be safe, put his sword away. Once more he held her in his arms and told her, "'Behold, I tell you a mystery: We shall not all sleep, but we shall all be changed – in a moment, in the twinkling of an eye, at the last trumpet.' And God will wipe away every tear from their eyes; *there shall be no more death, nor sorrow, nor crying.* This will not be the end, Pandora." With the hem of his cloak, he dabbed at her tears, doing his best to comfort her.

Her mind was in chaos after years of underground incarceration . . . even if she couldn't remember any of it. In spite of it all, somehow his words soothed her, if only a little.

Elias rose and stared down the Reaper. "Long ago you claimed my shadow – if it is time for my flesh then so be it."

Death responded in a way Elias wasn't expecting – he couldn't put his finger on it, but there was an indescribable reaction from the black-robed creature.

Slowly the ominous master of demise raised its arm and pointed to the papers on the floor with its black-stained bony finger poking from its tattered robe.

What are you trying to tell me? Elias wondered.

Death remained motionless, patiently waiting as if it had all eternity.

Elias reached down to grab the papyrus sheets – Byron was trying to tell him something else. He carefully read one sheet after the next. As he took in the information, finally reaching the last page and fully understanding the written words, his heart sank.

"No. NO! This cannot be," he exhaled in disbelief.

Pandora ran to his side. "What? What is it?"

"I . . . I was wrong. It is quite the opposite of what I thought."

"Opposite? You're not making any sense!"

"These pages from the Book of the Dead *are about me!* They are about this very moment in time, even though they were written at the base of the statue of Saint Longinus centuries ago. It was known this very moment would transpire . . . but it gets worse."

Pandora tightly grasped his metal-covered hand with her delicate fingers. "Go on."

"Death ripped away my shadow, but he never stole it."

Her eyes momentarily flickered. "That's a good thing, right?"

He shook his head, "Death only *separated* my shadow from body. I did in fact fall that day. Even now my body lies in that dark lonely pit, nothing more than rotting flesh and broken bones."

Her blood ran cold. "But . . . no! Then you are . . ."

The Black Knight removed his helmet, and Pandora *screamed* at the top of her lungs. What she saw was horrific. His eyes were gone, and he had no face – there was only a black emptiness within the armor.

"Yes. I did die. This is all that is left of me. *I am that shadow.*"

Pandora fell on the ground and backpedaled as quickly as she could. This wasn't Elias. It *couldn't* have been! She trembled in horror as she beheld the armored knight absent of flesh and bone. Where his head should've been was nothing more than a dark, hollow shadow. As her eyes focused, she noticed two red glowing eyes – the only part of him made up of anything other than utter darkness.

The shadow knight rose and turned to face Death, now understanding his fate and also resigned to it.

Despite her overwhelming fear, Pandora couldn't stand the thought of watching what was about to happen.

He was a shadow – he was undead. But he was her friend. Even more than that, he was the one that saved her.

Pandora looked in her hand at the Queen's Abandonment. The golden crown was no longer what it once was – her bloody hands clung to it no longer as a proclamation of riches, but only as a reminder of her failings. What was once glorious and in all of its splendor, the crown formerly known as the Queen's Heaven was stained an oily-black and missing its most magnificent diamond piece.

Abandonment. It was surely an abandonment.

But….

What Elias did for her. What the blood of Christ did for her. She was putting her hope in the wrong things, and it took her this long to finally figure that out.

"Please, God. Oh, please….I know I don't talk to you much, but I think I understand now. Forgive me, Lord! But please…. if there is a way to save Elias, I am begging you. Don't let him die….just *don't*!" she sobbed.

Death reached out to embrace a waiting Elias and wrap him into the folds of his cloak.

At that very moment, a blinding flash of light filled the entire cavern. Pandora gasped with awe, partially covering her eyes with her hands since she could barely see, daring to squint and peer through her fingers.

It was difficult to tell, but she could've sworn she saw *three* indistinguishable figures illuminated, two of which were black but swallowed by the brilliant luminescence. The third figure was dressed in white, so immaculate she wondered if he - or it - was the reason for the incandescent flood.

Her glimpse was brief. The radiant light was so overwhelming that she passed out.

***

Then spoke Jesus again to them, saying, I am the light of the world: he that follows me shall not walk in darkness, but shall have the light of life.

John 8:12

***

Neither Elias the Black Knight nor Pandora Seraphia were ever seen again.

Rumors persisted over the next several years as to what fate possibly befell the star-crossed couple.

Long before that, when Elias and Pandora first went missing, many from the orphanage rejoiced for their escape, believing the two ran away from their oppressive authorities, hoping against hope that they started their own lives together and far away from any adult.

There were only four orphans that didn't celebrate.

Hiram, Thomas, Tobias, and especially Samuel never spoke of what happened that one night they dared travel to Wraithfall Ruins. It was only guilt that prompted Hiram to tell the Headmistress that Elias and Pandora were last seen heading toward Wraithfall Ruins, but that was all he confessed.

A small party formed by the local sheriff investigated briefly, but their search turned up nothing – Elias and Pandora were never found.

What Lies Beneath Wraithfall Ruins

More recent stories speculated on the fate of the one known as the Black Knight. The general consensus among local townsfolk was that the Black Knight did, in fact, travel to Wraithfall Ruins – alone and out of sheer will – desperately seeking an answer to a great mystery. Some believed that the Black Knight split off from the Order of the Word, abandoning his God, choosing to seek an artifact of great power – and great evil. Others combined his legend with that of another: The girl who unleashed an unspeakable evil from deep underneath the ruins.

Those tales spoke of his quest to find her, the one living girl who remained trapped underground, but before he could find her he fell victim to the White Widow – and the girl is still trapped somewhere underneath to this day.

Some, if asked, believe that the knight *did* find the girl, but they both died a tragic death before they could escape from underground. However, due to their faithfulness to God, their souls were whisked away to heaven, rewarded for their suffering and devotion, finally able to live together under His holy light and grace in paradise for all eternity.

One of the less believed rumors claimed that the Black Knight was actually a shadow – perhaps a *living* one full of life and soul, remaining a Knight of the Word despite his great curse and working for the church as their work was not yet done, but conversely, quite possibly an *undead* shadow bound to obey and labor under the Reaper.

There was an old monk who disputed that rumor, insisting the Black Knight survived the ordeal despite staring down the Face of Death. He brought Pandora to a monastery high on Kings Mountain where she could recover and be prayed over, and the monk witnessed it all. The knight retired from the Order shortly after. Pandora became his bride and they left the monastery the following spring. They traveled as far as they could from the cursed countryside and built a house at the base of a quiet mountain, near a lake, where they made a home together and had many children.

Pandora never did regain her full memories of what happened to her underneath Wraithfall Ruins – she still had many restless nights, but she kept her Bible close, and the Black Knight was always there for her.

Whatever the truth may be, God only knows. But no soul will dispute that somewhere deep beneath Wraithfall Ruins, the White Widow still wails with hate, ravenous to feed on anyone foolish enough to come to her, burning in her hatred of all creatures blessed with the gift of life.

And they are right.

Impatiently she waits. The next child to stumble into her realm would not be so lucky. There would be *no* redemption – no escape. Even though the White Widow was imprisoned underneath Wraithfall Ruins, the draw to her was powerful, and there would always be a rebellious, sinful child that would answer her call.

It was just a matter of time.

Shadow Walkers

Elizabeth Alsobrooks

Shadow Walkers
Elizabeth Alsobrooks

Sabina jumped and glanced toward the heavy rosewood door. Someone pounded as though pursued by zombies. The dignified Westminster Chimes of her doorbell sounded next, and seemed unaffected by the alternate fist-pounding.

She slid open the drawer, grasped the revolver and curled her finger around the trigger.

"Sabina! Sabina! Let me in!"

Tessa. That explained why the doorman had let her up without phoning. Withdrawing her hand from the coffee table cubby, this time without the firearm Andrew insisted she learn to use and keep handy, Sabina ran to flip the deadbolt and pull the door open.

"Tessa! What's wrong?"

Tessa fairly exploded into the room, overwhelming Sabina with a swirl of canary chiffon and whiffs of soft floral. Her best friend's cheery adornment was in stark contrast to the ravaged look on her upturned oval face. Dark mascara ran down her ghostly pale face. Streaks were smudged across her high, sun-freckled cheekbones by repeated attempts, like the one she performed now, to still the rivulets of tears. "Oh, Sabina. Thank the goddess you are home," Tessa declared, throwing herself into Sabina's waiting arms and sobbing brokenly.

"Shhh. What has you so hysterical, Tess?" Sabina asked, trying to sound calm above Tessa's shuddering mass of soft copper curls, though her friend's unusual behavior terrified her, making her dread the answer to her own question. *Why didn't I call her earlier when I sensed something was wrong?*

She stiffened as her earlier premonition manifested into a sudden vision of Lydia, her six-year-old goddaughter and Tessa's only child, crouched in a dark room. *No, not a room, underground, chill, damp, earthen, a cavern of some kind.* She let herself be drawn into the psychic realm and was hit by a strong surge of acrid, sulfuric stench, though she saw no signs of fire or scorched wood. The air gave her goose flesh, and the smell didn't match the environment Lydia's tiny form occupied. As though sensing her presence, the little girl glanced over her shoulder and Sabina gasped, her chest tightening at the abject terror and bewilderment on the little tear-stained face, a miniature version of Tess.

Tessa drew back, her action pulling Sabina from her brief, trance-like state. Gone was her friend's usually composed and sophisticated demeanor. She stared pleadingly into Sabina's eyes.

"Sabina--"

"We'll get Lydia back. I promise. Tell me everything you know."

Tessa didn't question how her friend's unexplained insight. She was used to Sabina's visions. Instead she blurted, "I-I-I've made a stupid mistake. I did everything he said. Everything. If-if I thought Lydia was in danger I would have sent her away, to my mother or my sister, Gena, in Spain."

"Okay, focus, honey. It's me, Sabina. You're like my sister. I know you would never put Lydia in harm's way. Tell me the facts and start with who this *he* is, what he had you doing, and why you agreed to do it."

"Mr. Cardiff. He came to the art gallery one day and purchased a rare original we had just gotten in, so of course I thought he was a serious collector. When he asked me to find other, specific work, I was happy to comply. Everything was normal and he became a high-priority client very quickly. Why wouldn't he? How could I have known?"

"I don't see that you did anything wrong here, honey. What is it you should have known?"

Tessa nodded and took a deep breath. She squared her shoulders and seemed to get control of her emotions. "Everything was fine, but then he wanted me to find some unusual and highly controversial pieces, expensive and dear to the perverted collectors who seek them, true, but not the sort of work our gallery deals with, and I told him so."

"Controversial how?"

"Twisted, degenerate garbage, from Bloody demonic rites to perversion with children, the sort of erotica collected by perverts such as Le Marquis De Saud."

"He asked you to find them for him?"

"Quite specifically, by artist and title. Things sold only on the black market by the sort of sick bastards who traffic in child slavery or splatter films involving kidnapped young victims to sadists with deep enough pockets to fund their thirst for torture, rape and murder."

"Oh, Tess. You said you did all he demanded. You don't mean to say that you were trafficking in child pornography? These are the people who have Lydia? What do they want? Why have they taken her?"

"Of course not! He asked a few times, very politely, and each time I turned him down. He seemed very casual about it, but a week would pass and he would ask again. Yesterday he rang me up and asked me to host a showing of this material at the gallery, a night showing by invitation only with work he would provide himself. Of course I refused. It would have ruined the business, and I had no intention of hosting a party for the type of people who'd be interested in this sort of exhibition. He pretended to go along with my refusal, even said he understood, but when I went in to wake Lydia this morning she was gone. She was just missing, and there were no signs of a break-in."

"Did you call the police?"

"No," Tess said, taking a deep breath to calm herself. "Just as I reached for the phone it rang, as if he could actually *see* me. He told me if I called the police, Lydia would never come home and he would find her some very willing playmates." She shuddered and added softly, "I knew exactly what he meant. I have no doubt he means what he said."

"So in order to get her back, he wants you to host a gala for illegal pornography?"

"Yes."

"When?" Sabina asked, knowing Tess would do as Lydia's abductor demanded.

"Tomorrow night."

"So soon," Sabina said, her mind rushing for a solution. *There was no time to get help from Andrew. He couldn't arrive home by then.*

She'd have to help Tessa herself, aided only by outrage.

And magic.

***

Chill air permeated her light summer tank top. Sabina massaged her arms to smooth the bumps raised from more than the temperature. Backed against the wall, she flashed her torch into the thick black of the tunnel ahead, unable to find anything, including her earlier bravado.

She had recognized the catacombs in her vision and knew Lydia was being held there, but the only route she knew by heart was the one Andrew had taught her, the one that led to the Vatican.

Light bounced over the surface of loose stones and stray footprints that may have been created centuries ago in the dusty walkway. Natural rock was interspersed with crumbling, ancient archways and chambers erected by secretive societies, some Christian, others pagan, depending upon the era and location, but all neglected and abandoned. The result was an uneven and jagged surface, casting strange, dubious reflections within the beam's reach.

Where in all this maze of tunnels was Lydia?

She sensed a presence, though none revealed itself.

Andrew called them shades because they could became virtual shadows, hidden from view and most often only discerned by a peripheral flash of movement, gone when one turned to look. Those that hid themselves in locations such as this were most likely vile, conniving and dangerous shapeshifters.

So what was she thinking to go against them?

Not waiting for Andrew hadn't been very smart, but she didn't know where he was at the moment. His last call came from Egypt. He had just arrived from Brazil and he'd mentioned that he might have to join his siblings, Luc and Kirin, who were off in America, on business for his mother.

Turning to look back down the tunnel, she assured herself there was no movement behind Tessa, who so far had remained quiet as promised. She'd never been this far underground before, and her heightened sense of danger urged her to turn and flee, but she was determined to find the fiend's lair, and Lydia.

That sweet little girl isn't going to be a pawn of these bastard jinn if I can do anything to prevent it, she vowed. She rubbed the talisman around her neck and softly chanted a protection spell. If only Tess had told her about the terror she'd been living sooner. Why had her best friend thought she could battle the jinn alone?

Wait, isn't that what I'm doing? she reminded herself. Of course, Tess didn't know she was up against jinn. Sabina didn't want her any more hysterical than she already was, so hadn't told her.

Too late to back out now. Taking a deep breath, she started down the corridor despite the growing sensation that they were being watched. Moments later, she came to a defile. The rock wall on the right was cracked from top to bottom. She crept to the edge of the fissure and peered into the gloom. The acrid scent of sulfur assaulted her on a rush of hot air. Gone was the chill and dampness of her vision. A jinni had been here, and recently.

Swallowing, she clambered through the hollow channeled into the rock wall. The beam from her torch dimmed and went out as though the brand new batteries were drained.

Sabina shook it until it flickered and regained a dim light, strong enough to scan the chamber. A pile of human skulls erected as though it were a shrine rose in the corner and gave her pause. Moving the light upward, she saw that the wall was literally mortared with the macabre human bricks, as were many other walls within the catacombs.

This would be a terrifying place for a child, she thought, just as she spotted a small, stooped figure near the far wall, huddled beneath a shelf-like depression where a few bone fragments were all that remained of a once prominent corpse whose tomb had been desecrated centuries ago.

Sabina started toward it. "Lydia? Is that you, honey?" she called softly.

"Lydia! Oh my baby," Tessa cried, pushing past Sabina and running toward the young girl who, spotting her, jumped up and ran to meet her.

"Oh, mommy, you came, you came. I want to go home," the child whispered brokenly, glancing fearfully toward the room's original doorway, a large arch to the right of where they had entered. It led to yet another passageway. Lydia grasped her mother around the waist and buried her face against her stomach.

Sabina rushed forward to embrace her friend and goddaughter. "Come on, we have to go. Now!"

"Oh, yes, mommy, yes, we have to go before one of those monsters comes back," Lydia readily agreed and began tugging on her mother's arm.

"Monsters? What--"

"Now, mommy. Hurry!"

Understanding Lydia's terror, Sabina needed no urging and led the way out of the crevice. Shielding their presence with a quick spell, she ran as fast as Lydia could keep up. They turned a corner in the catacomb tunnels, and Sabina stopped so abruptly that first Lydia and then Tessa ran into her.

She threw her arms out to stop them from stepping around her and then raised her arms, palms forward and chanted three times, "Goddess surround us with a shield of protection and keep us safe within this space."

Tessa and Lydia grouped up tight against her back and she could feel when Tessa half-turned to watch behind them.

The jinni blocking their path inched closer, his head tilting as he tried to see behind her. She clearly wasn't his target. He probably had orders to capture Lydia and Tessa without harm. No doubt he considered her nothing more than an insignificant obstacle to be removed.

Lydia trembled against her back, and she heard a smothered sob as the child tried to contain her terror. A protective impulse strengthened Sabina's resolve. The stench from the shadow walker forced her to breathe from her mouth. Her eyes watered in response to both the smell and escalating heat radiating from the ashy being. It resembled a live ember with a man-like shape. Its outer skin was sooty yet undulated around a lava-like core which was revealed in glowing instances as the creature moved its massive body. It reached out an arm-like appendage and swiped at her, only to come up against the protection barrier.

The shifter paused. It studied her more closely as though reevaluating her threat-potential. Sweat beaded on her forehead. Sabina clenched and then reopened her hands, palms facing the hideous beast. She quickly channeled energy, more concerned that reinforcements would arrive than that the single fledgling entity, however dangerous, would penetrate the protection shield she'd created.

Drawing power from the earth, she centered her focus and urged green magic up her body, into her hands, and outward toward the jinni. Mouthing a word of power and calling out to the goddess, she projected energy. Green-tinged white light beams shot from her hands into the beast's core. Roaring in anger and pain, it was slammed into the rock wall flailing for only a moment before it erupted. A burst of sparks careened against their protective barrier, the walls and ceiling, and then drifted to the ground, extinguished. All that remained was scattered ash.

Without hesitation, Sabina glanced behind her and said, "Run, more will have heard and be coming!"

"What the hell was that thing?" Tessa cried out.

"A jinni. Now let's go."

"A jinni? But you said they were like wispy shadows."

"Monsters," Lydia whispered fearfully.

"What you just saw is their true form. They shapeshift into anything they wish, but most often travel secretly among us as shadow walkers. Come on, Tess, I mean it, we have to go!"

She pushed back a sudden craving for espresso and ran, despite the sluggishness her brief battle and adrenaline wane had left her with.

They neared a cross-tunnel she remembered from her way down through the catacombs and slowed. Glancing to her right, she splashed her torch light down the yawning gap in the rock wall. Nothing. She turned her head toward the left and sensed a presence just before a shadow flickered in her peripheral, to the left. Jerking her light to the tunnel on her other side, she searched for the jinni, but saw nothing.

Just behind her, Lydia caught up. She heard the child gasp before she stumbled and fell. Her mother rushed forward and reached to help her to her feet.

"Are you okay?" Sabina asked, turning in a slow circle, but unable to find the source of her disquiet.

Lydia reached down and brushed ineffectively at the dust on the white linen nightgown she had been wearing when abducted. Sabina had gifted it to her on a shopping spree a few weeks ago. It was badly stained and trailing a length of torn white lace. The tiny pink rosebuds scattered playfully across the bodice were barely distinguishable upon the filthy fabric.

When the young girl didn't respond, Sabina said, "Lydia, honey, are you okay?"

"Yes," she said, glancing up at Sabina. "Just tripped. Can we go home now?"

Sabina noticed a small scorch mark on the edge of the child's gown, frowned, and said, "I'm getting us out of here right now, sweetheart. I promise."

She placed her hand upon Lydia's head and smoothed the strawberry-blond curls, forcing a reassuring smile. Then she turned back to the tunnel, a sudden, urgent plan forming in her mind as she abruptly changed directions and continued to lead the way through the labyrinth of tunnels.

***

Finding the door she sought at last, Sabina disabled the lock with a push of green magic and swung the metal gate, banging on a thick wooden door. She had no idea who was on the other side, or whether anyone was close enough to even hear her, but they were getting in, one way or another.

"We seek sanctuary," she called out.

"Where are we?" Tess asked, clearly frightened.

"I'm getting us to safety," Sabina said.

Before she could explain further, the door swung open on well-oiled hinges.

"How did you get here? Who are you? You need to return the way you came. This isn't an exit and you have no business here. Do I need to phone the authorities and have you arrested?"

"Take us to Father Benjamin. It's urgent."

When the priest would have objected further, Sabina turned and lifted waves of thick raven hair to expose the molten gold starburst within the eye of Ra, a small tattoo at the base of her neck. Andrew had insisted she receive the small protection symbol. Recognized by all members of his influential family's organization, the rune identified her as a trusted insider who must be aided and protected without question. She had experienced its usefulness twice before when some strange men had tried to accost her. Both times she had run to the Vatican for help as Andrew had instructed her. His family had powerful friends, but equally ruthless enemies.

"Inside, quickly," the priest said without further argument. He stepped back to let them enter, then hurried down the steps and refastened the heavy padlock.

Watching him, Sabina noticed a slight movement on the inside of the archway above the gate. A security camera. Of course. Someone had known the moment they arrived. The clergyman slid a rough timber through iron slots and turned an antique key worn around his neck into a large keyhole in the door. Surprised by the antiquated security, Sabina glanced up and noted another security camera, which looked oddly out of place in the ancient chamber mortared with raw boulders.

The priest turned and rushed them to a door at the opposite side of the chamber. It was opened by another cleric, and as they stepped into a long hallway, a half-dozen black-robed young men who looked rather burly to be priests, separated to let them pass.

Travertine tiles paved the floor within the narrow, stacked stone hallway. Their escort didn't pause to speak to the men who'd obviously been waiting should he need assistance, but instead led them through a labyrinth of similar hallways, twice requiring them to go through locked doors and once up a flight of uneven, worn stone stairs.

The priest stopped before a red door and when he pulled it open, Sabina was surprised to see an elevator. The group entered and rode upward, still silent and tense. When the cables stilled, they stepped out and followed the priest across the hall. This time when he opened a set of double doors, he moved aside and said, "Please feel free to get cleaned up. I will have some refreshments and clean clothing sent up at once. Father Benjamin will be with you as soon as we can get word to him. In the meantime, you are safe here."

Before Sabina could reply, he spun on his heels and was on his way back to the elevator, a cell phone to his ear. She closed and locked the doors.

***

By the time Tessa bundled Lydia into one towel and rubbed water from her hair with another, a young cleric had provided clean clothes for them all. The delivery contained simple summer shifts for the women, a white jumper for Lydia, and store-packaged underwear. Though not the most flattering styles, because Sabrina suspected the serviceable clothing was kept on site and intended to fit a variety of female sizes in emergency situations, the garments were clean and comfortable and they were thankful for the kindness.

Sabina, showered and groomed, took a bite of the savory omelet another cleric had just provided and watched with growing alarm as Lydia shoveled cornflakes so fast the milk dripped from her chin and soggy flakes clung to the sides of her mouth.

"Slow down, honey. I know you're starving, but you will make yourself sick if you eat so fast," Tessa said, running her hand over Lydia's damp curls and smiling, seemingly too happy to have her safe to be concerned by her daughter's behavior.

She hadn't let the child out of her sight since they recovered her, and had repeatedly thanked Sabina. That seemed understandable, but what Tessa hadn't done was ask a dozen more questions about the jinn as soon as they were safe, and Sabina found that to be as odd as the fact that Lydia was now grabbing handfuls of cereal from the bowl and jamming them into her mouth until her checks resembled a chipmunk.

A knock sounded as Tessa finally grabbed Lydia's hand with alarm and said, "Lydia, stop that this minute!"

Sabina hurried from the small sitting room, wondering what lasting trauma her godchild faced. The supposedly locked left door suddenly opened, allowing a hooded Jesuit to step into the suite's antechamber. Ignoring her, he rushed past her toward the sound of shattering glass followed by Tessa's shocked cry of, "Lydia! What are you doing?"

Sabina followed close behind the man's billowing robes and stopped beside him, just in time to duck. A coffee cup projectile hit the threshold from across the length of the room from the small dining table near the balcony doors. Watching the cup shatter, her sweet godchild laughed and then began to throw silverware with such force, more force than her six-year-old arm could possibly muster, it protruded, wobbling like windblown tinsel, from the thick plaster walls. The reverberation still ringing in her ears, Sabina shouted, "Lydia! Stop it at once!"

Instead of the usual contrite expression at her Aunty Sabina's scolding, Lydia pounding her little fists on the table until the plates rattled. When Tess reached to grasp her daughter's arm, Lydia twisted away, jumping from her chair and screaming, "No! Leave me alone!"

She fled to the end of the table where she was abruptly caught up in the arms of the cleric who lifted her from her feet and swung her into a semi-circle in order to plant her firmly in the chair closest to him. When she would have sprung back up, the gentle push of his hands on her shoulders stilled her motion.

"Stay still, child." Turning toward Sabina he said, "Hand me the phone."

Confused, she handed him her cell phone only to have him motion it away and demand, "The desk phone!"

Still baffled, she hurried to the desk and grabbed the phone.

When she handed it to him, he made a sound of disgust, dropped the wireless receiver and darted past her. She watched in alarm as he reached down to pull the cord from the wall, and then snapped it out of the stand. He hurried back and began wrapping the cord around Lydia's right forearm, binding it to the chair arm.

"Wait, what do you think you're doing?" Tessa cried out.

Sabina grabbed his sleeve and cried, "Let her go!"

He jerked his arm away and snapped, "It's not me that's got her!"

They both stepped back in surprise as the chair suddenly levitated four feet into the air, out of Tessa's reach.

"Sabina!" Tessa grabbed an arm of the chair, the one without the child's arm tied to it. She pulled, trying to lower Lydia back to the floor.

Alarmed, Sabina pulled on a chair leg. Lydia laughed with delight at her unexplainable ride.

"Get her down, Sabina!" Tessa begged.

Sabina spoke a spell and the chair returned to the floor.

"A sorceress? Good. Then stop using your emotions and use your senses. You know as well as I do what needs to be done. Now help me do it!" Father Benjamin ordered.

Sabina, confused, didn't respond.

"Do you want to help me or wait for integration?"

Integration? Sabina froze and took several deep breaths in order to calm. Then it hit her. An overwhelming sense of malevolent darkness. *It's here. Right here. Right , . . oh my God, no! Lydia is possessed by a jinn, and if we don't make it leave her body soon, she might suffer irreparable mental damage.*

"What can I do? Tessa, get back."

"Sabina, what are you saying? Help me. Help me untie Lydia."

"She's put *herself* there, Tess. That is, not her but the jinni who has possessed her."

"What are you talking about? That's crazy. Are you trying to tell me my baby is possessed by a demon?"

"Not a demon, a jinn, but the possession is similar. Father Benjamin is an expert on jinn as well as demons, which is why I asked for his help."

"How long, do you know how long it's had her?" asked Father Benjamin, using his belt to tie her other arm to the chair.

"Not long," she said. "A couple hours, since just before we arrived, in the tunnels on the way here."

"Good," the priest said. "It'll be easier then. It hasn't had a chance to latch on tight yet."

Tess began to sob. "Oh, my baby. Please, save her, father. Should I get a crucifix or something?"

"It's a jinni, not a demon, Tess. Just please, honey, stay out of his way."

Tessa backed away, her hands clasped tightly to her chest. "P-please, just help her."

"You must be so proud of yourself," Father Benjamin said, mocking the jinni within Lydia. "Unremarkable among your brethren, a minion, able to capture and hold an escaped prisoner. A child, yes, but you still captured her all by yourself. So what's your name, since you're so brave?"

"It's not going to be that easy, priest." It wasn't Lydia's voice and the sardonic laugh that followed in no way resembled the bubbly giggle of a six-year-old girl.

They were still staring at Lydia in horror when she suddenly vanished. The chair crashed over backward, the belt and phone cord—now loose without Lydia's arms bound within—still tied to the now empty chair.

"It never is," muttered the priest as he untangled his belt from the chair and replaced it around his waist.

"Where did she go?" cried Tessa, rubbing her hand across the chair's seat as though Lydia might just be invisible, as if that were preferable to missing altogether.

"Dammit! I should have bound him here. Sorry, father," Sabina added, referring to her cursing.

"You damn sure should have," he said. "But it's my fault too. I assumed you had, and I should have pointed it out to you, to be sure."

"What can I do to help?" Sabina asked, reaching out to grasp his arm.

"Unless you already know her whereabouts, wouldn't a locator spell be the best place to begin our search?" Father Benjamin suggested.

"Yes, do it, Sabina. What if he's taken her back to where the rest of those monsters are?" Tessa urged.

"Yes, quickly, I can only sense them for a short time and distance. I might lose the trail by the time we reach the tunnels, which I believe is where they did indeed go. Thank you, Senorita," said the Spanish priest.

***

Boots on stone, muffled but recognizable, could be heard in a side-tunnel ahead. Father Benjamin stopped and raised his hand, signaling to Sabina and Tessa.

Sabina chanted a protection spell to boost the shield she'd already erected around them. She reached for Tessa's hand. It was moist and trembled slightly, so she squeezed it with reassurance.

Faint torch-light announced the first of the approaching group in the junction ahead of them. Tessa huddled against the wall. Sabina moved closer, warning her friend with the press of her hand not to scream and instantly alert the newcomers to their presence.

But then something familiar drew Sabina's attention to the tallest man, out in front, confidence clear in both his stride and carriage. The breadth of his shoulders, his gait, the way he turned his head and a strand of hair fell down over his forehead, all familiar. He reached up to shove his hair behind his ear and Sabina rushed forward. When Father Benjamin grabbed her arm, she called out, "Andrew! Andrew, it's me. I'm here!"

"What are you doing, Senorita?"

Pulling herself free of the cleric's grasp, she ran toward her lover's open arms.

"Sabina, what are you doing here, love?" Andrew demanded, catching her up against himself for a fierce hug and then a kiss.

Pulling back, Sabina said, "I don't know why you're here, but I've never been happier to see you."

"I know why," shouted Father Benjamin. Towing Tessa behind him, he urged them all back into the tunnel behind Andrew. "Sabina, throw up a protection shield. A strong one. Now!"

His urgent tone was all the motivation she needed. Raising her arms, she closed her eyes to help her focus and began to chant. Soon, a greenish mist rose up from the floor to block the tunnel, just as a swirling mass of black shadows arrived. They sparked against her barricade in a futile attempt to reach the humans just beyond their grasp, then retreated to regroup and come up with another strategy. Sabina relaxed and took a deep breath.

"More? More jinn?" Tessa cried. "How will we reach my baby now?"

Andrew glanced down at Tessa. "Lydia? Are you saying they have your daughter?"

"One of them possessed her," Sabina explained as Tessa burst into tears.

Andrew looked to one of his men. With a nod, he indicated that Tessa should be removed from the catacombs. "Tell my mother that she is a guest who must be kept from leaving for her own safety."

When Tessa tried to protest, Sabina said, "Please, Tessa. Go with him. You need to be protected too." Her hysterics would hinder their progress in getting her daughter back.

Father Benjamin placed his hands upon Tessa's shoulders. Looking down at her with the most compassion Sabina had yet seen him demonstrate, he said softly, "It's for the best, Senora. I will bring the child back to you myself. You have my word."

Finding comforting strength in the man's gaze, Tessa stopped sobbing, nodded her resignation and turned to accompany Andrew's man.

Once Tessa was out of sight, Sabina gave Andrew a brief rundown on what had occurred. He listened calmly, and then said, "You should have called me, Sabina. My mother's intelligence people monitor everything that happens in the city. Knowing that, didn't you realize she would send for me once this number of jinn were discovered in one place? Lydia might have become an innocent victim if we hadn't run into you first." Even more foreboding in the shadowy torchlight, his jaw, manly and strong, usually one of his most handsome features, looked to be made of granite.

Sabina shrugged. "Weren't you going to fetch Father Benjamin anyway?" He made a small sound of irritation. No doubt her resisted the urge to send her after Tessa but hesitated only because he knew how helpful her magic could be against the jinn.

To keep her own fiery temper in check at his chastisement, all the more irritating because he was right, she reached up to kiss his chin and defuse his mood. Her handsome, dark-haired love shook his head at her impudence and chuckled.

When he put his arm around her waist and gave a quick squeeze, growling "Let's get this done then," she smiled, knowing that she and his beloved brother, Luc, were the only people who could coax him out of a foul mood. How could she be annoyed with him when he was only concerned for her safety and getting her godchild rescued before she came to harm.

"I assume since you're here, you've brought what I need, my Prince?" Father Benjamin interrupted.

Sabina didn't miss Andrew's brief concern that she'd heard the priest address him as prince. How could he think that after more than a decade together, she didn't know his secrets? She was a sorceress. Could he possibly believe she wouldn't know about his mother, Queen Isis, the most powerful of all her kind? They needed to have a serious conversation sooner than later, but for now they had more pressing issues to address.

He gestured to a man whose face was familiar because he was so often disrupting their dinners or lunches to whisper an urgent message in Andrew's ear—a message that usually meant he would have to cut their date short. This man, Giovani, and his driver, Michael, never Mike, were always with them, even waiting close by when they spent the night together. "Give it to the priest," Andrew said.

Father Benjamin took a wrapped object from Giovani. He removed the fabric, placed it on the ground at his feet, setting the silver chalice it contained in its center.

"The Chalice of Isis?" she murmured reverently, gazing at the legendary artifact in awe. Even in the dim light of their torches the polished silver gleamed, and its etched engravings sparkled. Its presence filled her with renewed confidence in their success.

"You recognize it?" Andrew asked in surprise.

She gave him a sidelong look that bespoke the volumes of things she knew that he shouldn't take for granted. He wisely let the subject drop.

Father Benjamin unpacked a bag she hadn't noticed he'd slung over his shoulder and began to dump a variety of vial contents into the bowl while chanting an ancient spell she recognized but didn't know by heart as he apparently did. This time, she was surprised. Though Andrew had told her if she ever needed metaphysical help she should ask for Father Benjamin, she had no idea he was a practitioner of magic. She began to doubt he was actually a priest in any modern sense of the word, for his abilities had their roots in much older arts.

"Don't look so surprised," he said, startling her.

"I-I, that is, I didn't realize," she said.

"We've not had a witch burning in some time," the priest said, laughing for the first time since she'd met him.

"I know of this spell," Sabina said. "You call it forth from thousands, not hundreds of years ago, holy man."

"Si, Senorita," he said, once again sober. "As you say. Now, we've quite a host to subdue. I could use your help, Sorceress."

"As you wish," she said. "Andrew, we need vessels that seal."

Anticipating the request, Giovani stepped forward and began handing her and Father Benjamin cork-sealed ceramic vases. They pulled out the stoppers and lined the vessels up beside the chalice.

"Are you ready?"

She nodded, and he said, "Release the shield."

Sabina raised her arms and spoke the words. Almost at once the shadowy jinn began to move toward them from the adjacent tunnel. Sabina could smell their sulfuric stench and was glad when Father Benjamin added frankincense to the chalice and then lit the entire contents. Flame shot upward and they took a step back as billows of green smoke spread out into the intersection.

"Now," he told her. Together they began to chant. She followed his lead and they were soon repeating the ancient phrases in unison.

Realizing their intent, the jinn screeched in outrage, the sound both hideous and deafening as it echoed through the tunnels. An explosion sounded. Sabina gasped. Battery-powered torches the men were carrying cracked and went out. The passageway grew dimmer, but not dark. She was glad the men had the foresight to bring flaming torches as well. At least the creatures couldn't suck their energy and cause them to explode.

They chanted louder, both to focus and drown out the unnatural din.

Father Benjamin reached to remove the cork from a vessel. He raised his arms and with the downward sweep of his hands he shouted, "Inside, deviant creature. I bind you. I bind you to this shape and this vessel. I bind you!" A spiraling, wailing black cloud of smoke descended toward them and slipped into the vessel. Sabina grabbed another container and uncorked it. As Father Benjamin sealed the fate of the first shifter, she pulled in the next.

They took turns until no more shape shifters appeared, all sucked toward the chalice and into Father Benjamin's power.

Andrew and a half-dozen men ran through the intersection and into the tunnels beyond. Sabina cast a protection spell over the trapped jinn, in case others showed up, returning from various missions, and tried to free them.

"Search for Lydia and bind her, Sabina. We can't let that jinni take her out of here," said Father Benjamin.

Sabina chanted a locator spell and focused. Finding the girl, she said, "She's back where we first found her, but she's not alone." She continued to focus, "Andrew and two of his men are headed right toward them! We have to go!"

They ran through the intersection and down the tunnel from which she had earlier led Lydia and Tessa, the one Andrew and two of his men had chosen. Pushing a spell to bind Lydia to her current location sapped her strength. Sabina paused to lean against the wall, panting.

"Here, drink this." Father Benjamin handed her a bottle of water.

Gulping until she had to take another breath, she gasped, "What is this?"

"I added a little rejuvenation to the water to make it more effective in such situations," the monk said, evasively.

She did indeed feel less exhausted, so she took another few gulps before handing it back. "I'd forgotten how physically draining magic use can be."

"Do you feel able to move on?"

"Yes, but I must try to push a shield around Andrew. He always thinks his brute force is all he needs for protection." *Though he has a magic of his own, too, perhaps given to him by his mother.*

"And immortality is helpful," Father Benjamin muttered to himself as he rushed down the tunnel, leaving her to catch up to him this time.

"What?"

"Nothing, just talking to myself."

Sabina paused to chant a protection shield around Andrew. He needed it more than she did at the moment. He was nearly upon the beast. Satisfied that he would be safe until she arrived, she took a deep breath and jogged onward, more slowly this time, but still ignoring her exhaustion.

She heard voices raised in agitation and a definite growl before she finally turned a corner in the tunnel and saw the fissure in the rock wall. Father Benjamin stood at the entrance to the chamber in which they'd found Lydia, chanting a spell she couldn't make out. She rushed forward and saw sparks.

"What's happening?" she asked, colliding with him in her haste to see into the chamber. He took a step sideways, allowing her to see the carnage unfolding as he continued chanting.

Lydia began screaming, or, rather, the jinn inside her was screaming. Father Benjamin's name and a string of profanity came out of the creature-controlled child's mouth. More sparks flew as Andrew beat back an enormous monstrosity, using a gleaming sword enshrouded in bluish-green flames. It was obviously enchanted.

The creature feared it.

The jinni couldn't be killed with firearms and something was special about the sword, making it lethal to their kind.

Tendril-like appendages arched outward from elongating extremities in an attempt to encircle and entrap Andrew with the lava-centered black webs. Sabina immediately raised her hands and spoke words of power, drawing the earth's energy upward through her body and projecting it toward the threat. Green-white bolts of lightning shot from the palms of each hand into the snaking tendrils. The jinni bellowed in outrage, writhing in pain.

Before the creature could retract its electrified tendrils, Andrew swung the sword and severed first one and then the other cluster of tangled coils. They fell to the ground, burning, and exploded into ash.

Sabina collapsed to her knees, drained.

"Sabina!" Andrew cried in alarm.

"I'm fine," she said, waving him away.

Behind them the evil being that held Lydia captive finally succumbed to Father Benjamin's magic. No longer able to possess its host, it fled, but it was bound to the cavern so didn't get far. It circled the chamber and finally settled for a spot in the corner, perched upside down on the ceiling, resembling a demonic dog that had been forged from charcoal dipped in black slime, the swirling lava interior still visible between its ribs, beneath its cheekbones and burning a fiendish, reddish-orange from its eye sockets.

Pungent sulfuric fumes permeated the chamber, and Sabina coughed, her eyes tearing as she crawled forward, reaching for Lydia's small, prone form. The child had collapsed, unconscious, once free of her evil captor.

Sparks flew, followed by a hideous scream of pain. Sabina plunged forward to throw herself over Lydia, chanting a spell that immediately shielded them. She glanced to the corner in time to see Andrew run his blade through the falling jinni, the height of the chamber no match for Andrew's 6' 8" reach.

Fiery movement from behind reminded her that the monstrous leader still lived. Hearing Father Benjamin chanting, she pushed more power into the shield. She shook Lydia's shoulder. Though there were no outward signs of physical damage discernable in the chamber's fluctuating light, who knew what lasting harm her godchild could suffer psychologically?

"Lydia, baby, wake up for your Aunty Sabina," she coaxed, patting the little girl's pale cheeks.

"Stop him, Father," Andrew shouted in warning. Sabina felt a violent force attacking the shield. She pushed back with the last of her energy, trying to pull more up from the earth to assist her. The monster bouncing off the walls with increased velocity colliding with her shield and she grit her teeth, closing her eyes against the salty perspiration running from her forehead. Yet another blow and she clenched her fists, struggling to hold on.

Andrew shouted again, but she couldn't make out what he said due to the increased ringing in her ears. She felt Lydia move and looked down to a weak smile lift the corners of her mouth. Smiling back took more energy than she had in reserve. Sabina reached for the child's hand as she slumped over, unable to keep her eyes open.

***

She woke in an SUV with darkly tinted windows. A flask was thrust into her hand and she took a long draught before turning to hand it back to Father Benjamin in the back seat.

"Aunty Sabina, you're awake," Lydia said, from beside him. "Are you okay?"

"I'm fine, honey. How do you feel?"

"I'm hungry and I want my mom."

Sabina smiled, glad to know Lydia was feeling better.

"You'll have plenty of food and hugs in just a few moments because we have arrived," Andrew announced. He reached to grasp Sabina's hand. "Sit tight. I'll be right there to help you out."

Before she could protest, he hurried out his side of the car and ran around to open her door. He insisted on holding her arm as he led her to the open elevator.

The moment they entered the antechamber of the hidden, underground compound, Tessa ran toward them. "Lydia! My baby!"

"I'm not a baby, Mommy," she said, throwing herself into her mother's outstretched arms. "I missed you. And I'm hungry!"

Several servants arrived as the detail of guards who had accompanied Andrew disappeared into various doors off the antechamber. "Anything she wants. She deserves it, Angelique," Andrew instructed.

A young woman with shoulder length black hair, fringed bangs, smooth, olive skin wearing a short, beige shift with bright byzantine print fabric and gladiator sandals smiled brightly, bowed, and motioned for Lydia to accompany her.

"I'll go with her," Tessa said. She hurried to Sabina, gave her a hug and then did the same to Andrew. Turning to Father Benjamin, she instinctively reached out, hesitated, and then hugged him tightly. "You kept your promise. Thank you," she said.

The cleric reddened under their gathered attention and then pulled away. "You're most welcome, Senora. I'm just glad she's safe and sound and back with her mother, where she belongs."

"I have espresso ready and waiting, your highness, or would you prefer to shower first," asked a hyper little man wearing an embroidered *kufi*, a heavily embroidered *sherwani* jacket with matching pants and simple brown, leather socks.

"Espresso," Andrew said, and the man took off as though about to win a foot race.

Tessa hurried after Lydia and Sabina held tight to Andrew's arm as they accompanied Father Benjamin toward the door through which Hassidim, who Sabina had met previously, disappeared.

"Mm, espresso sounds so good right now," Andrew and Sabina said in unison. They laughed as they reached the doorway.

***

"Sabina, thank you so much for being here with me. After everything you've already done for me, I didn't even have the right to ask you," Tessa said.

"It's fine, Tess. I slept for 14 hours straight, even after the espresso. I'm great. You need me here, so there's nowhere else I'd be. Besides, Andrew and Father Benjamin are here."

"Father Benjamin is here? I didn't see him come in. Where is he?" Tessa asked, smoothing her hair and looking around the gallery.

"You're certainly very excited about seeing a cleric again, Tessa. You do know they're celibate, right?"

"Yes," Tessa said softly. "But for some reason I don't think Father Benjamin is a priest, a monk, or any other sort of religious affiliate bound by vows of celibacy."

"Why not?"

Tessa shrugged. "I'm not sure why." She turned to speak to the caterer. After the well-tailored Italian walked away, Tessa chuckled as a figure across the room caught her eye. "No way! Father Benjamin isn't that guy in the jeans and sweater with the sexy bum is he?"

Sabina laughed. "You really don't think he's a holy man, do you?"

"Do you think that's the bum of a celibate man?"

Sabina joined in Tessa's laughter, then glanced toward the entrance as she sensed another, darker presence.

"It's him. He's here, Tessa. Are you ready?"

"As ready as it's possible to be," she said, then took a deep breath, grabbed Sabina's hand and said, "No. I don't think I can go through with this. I can't believe this freak escaped from both Andrew and Father Benjamin in the catacombs."

Sabina gave her hand a squeeze. "I was there and I can't believe it either, honey, but Andrew said he's a soul-eater and they've dealt with them before. Come on, for Lydia. Let's go greet the sunshine boy," Sabina said, heading toward the entryway, her bravery a front for her friend. She dropped Tessa's hand before her friend noted how they were shaking.

"Wait, tell me what a soul-eater is," Tessa insisted.

Knowing it was no use to soften the truth with her stubborn friend, Sabina said, "They're like vampires, but they suck the souls from a sinner's body. The more evil a person is, the better their soul tastes to a soul-eater. The more power it gives them."

Tessa grabbed Sabina's arm and pulled her close. "This monster has eaten more than his share, apparently," she said. "This is all so crazy! How can we hope to defeat it, especially when it commands a host of minions? This is a bad idea."

They could both see the jinn from where they stood. Mr. Cardiff, as he called himself, had shape-shifted into a handsome thirty-something male around 6' 2" with broad shoulders and long legs. More than one woman had given him a once-over when he entered. His thick, wavy hair and neatly trimmed beard and mustache complimented full yet masculine lips, high cheekbones and a firm jawline. A bulkier man, also wearing a fashionable though less expensive suit, stood silently a few feet behind him. Presumably it was his driver, or body guard, or both. Mr. Cardiff ignored his presence and surveyed the room with the confidence that came from money and power.

Sabina looped her arm through Tessa's and gave a little tug to pull her along, "Smile. We have no choice if we want to make sure Lydia stays safe. She can't live in the Vargas lair forever, can she?"

"You're right. I'm sorry. I can do this. I can." She marched across the room to prove it, Sabina hurrying to keep up. Tessa greeted Mr. Cardiff with a wide if brittle smile. When he shook her hand the smile waivered a little, but Sabina saw panic in her eyes and worried that she might bolt when he grasped her shoulders and buzzed a kiss to each cheek. To her credit, she recovered quickly and introduced him to Sabina.

The man turned dove-gray eyes toward Sabina and froze for a fraction of a moment. The surprised recognition in his eyes was instantly masked and he smiled, extending his hand.

So, he did see me in the catacombs, Sabina thought. *He'll have no problem recognizing Andrew, that's for sure. I hope he stays out of sight until we manage to get him within the circle.*

"Another beautiful woman. It's a great pleasure, *Signorina.*"

She placed her hand in his, with regret, and he turned it to place a lingering kiss upon it. Sabina resisted the urge to jerk her hand away. Barely. "Thank you, Mr. Cardiff," she said, easing her hand from his grasp.

Signaling a nearby waiter, Tessa said, "Please, have a flask of champagne, Mr. Cardiff."

"Perhaps later. I'm anxious to see the treasures you ordered. Would you care to accompany me?"

Tessa was unable to maintain her smile at the mention of the debauched ink drawing, photographs and paintings that currently defamed the walls of her gallery.

"I'm afraid I have to check on the caterers, but please, take your time and enjoy yourself," Tessa said. "We've already sold 3 or 4 paintings."

"Marvelous. Let the caterers do their job, my dear. I wanted to discuss one of the paintings with you. I swear the model could have been your twin," he said, grasping Tessa's elbow and steering her toward the gallery room on the left. "I'll bring her back in a few moments, *Signorina,*" he said to Sabina.

He didn't wait for her reply, hurrying Tessa away. When Sabina would have accompanied them, his guard suddenly stepped in front of her and said, "*Scusami.* Could you show me to the *bagno, per favore?*"

Sabina quickly pointed out the restrooms, but when she turned back toward Tessa and Mr. Cardiff, they had already disappeared. The gallery was getting crowded. Apparently the jinn was hungry and knew a lot of evil, depraved souls. Frightened for Tessa, she hurried forward, then slowed as she saw Father Benjamin stroll through the archway, obviously keeping track of Tessa too.

"Okay, my love, this way," Andrew said, appearing at her side and grabbing her hand. "They're going to bring him to us."

***

Sabina stood in the shadows near the back of the gallery. The overhead lights were off and except for some display lighting over a few lewd paintings, the room was dim. Inky splashes of darkness provided amply hiding for the men Andrew had used to surround the circle of protection. Sabina prepared the circle, drawing the runes with chalk and outlining the circle with salt. The chalice stood on a small altar at its center, already prepared by Father Benjamin.

Voices approached, and she heard Father Benjamin say, "I think I will be adding several pieces to my collection. I can't wait to see what you have in the reserve gallery. Your taste is superb, Mr. Cardiff. And you've done a great job of putting this showing together, Tessa."

Cardiff chuckled, but Tessa remained silent. A moment later the trio stepped through the archway into the back gallery. The moment they did, Sabina and Father Benjamin began to chant.

Looking first at the man he had mistaken for an illegal porn connoisseur, and then around the room, he spotted Sabina and cursed. Cardiff spun around to flee, but came up against the barrier Sabina erected. Green sparks showered those closest and everyone moved away from the shield blocking the only way in or out of the small rear gallery.

Father Benjamin ran to the chalice and lit the ingredients. As bluish-green smoke rose toward the ceiling, Sabina channeled more energy and encircled the raging jinn. Andrew and his men surrounded it, each armed with a blue-flaming sword. They were taking no chances this time.

Cardiff burst into flames as the soul-eater revealed its true self. The fine clothing settled to the floor as ash and the jinni screeched as it flailed against its confinement.

The priest recited an ancient spell in a lost language unfamiliar to Sabina and the jinni changed to a swirling mass of black and red-orange smoke. "Release it. Now, Sabina," cried Father Benjamin.

She reversed the spell and lifted the shield.

The angry entity struggled against the magic that drew it toward the chalice, but it was unable to resist the force exerted upon it by both Sabina and the cleric. It drew closer and Sabina watched as it twisted and turned, struggling against the pull.

"Where's the vessel?" Sabina asked.

"No need!" Andrew shouted, swinging his sword and swiping the cloudy mass in two.

Sparks flew. A gruesome shriek echoed around the small room. The creature exploded in a fireball of foul-smelling debris. Spinoff black shrouds of vapor circled the dying jinni, but they didn't vaporate. Instead they darted about the room until one after another began sparking against the shield in the archway.

"*Dios mío*. Those are souls. Evil souls," the priest said, crossing himself and kissing the crucifix hanging from his neck.

"Then let's send them to hell," Andrew said. "A little help, gentlemen!"

Andrew and his men moved in on the shadowy apparitions. With each swipe of an enchanted sword, another soul let out a mournful, hideous cry and vanished. As the last shriek drifted away, Andrew said, "Sabina, lift the shield. We need to get the rest of his minions. Be sure to seal the gallery so none escape."

Sabina dropped her attention from the rear gallery and focused on blocking the exits. Once she had the shields in place, she glanced around the room at the scattered piles of ash and noticed Tessa, plastered to the wall, frozen in terror.

"Oh, come here, Tess. It's going to be okay now, I promise," Sabina said, holding her arms out as Tessa stumbled toward her, clearly in shock. She only hoped she hadn't lied to her friend.

***

It was dusk by the time Lydia finished her gelato and the women finished their espressos. Sabina walked with them to the curb and gave them each a heartfelt hug. Things had returned to normal over the past few weeks, and the trio had spent a delightful afternoon shopping for Lydia's school clothes, and of course a brand new white cotton nightgown with tiny rosebuds.

Fastening Lydia's seatbelt, Sabina gave her a quick kiss on the cheek. "A bath and straight to bed, young lady. I won't want your mom to scold me for getting you that gelato so close to bedtime."

"I will. I promise, Aunty Sabina. Thank you for the lovely presents."

"You've most welcome, honey." Standing to close the door, she waved. Tessa rolled down the window. "I had a great time with you girls today, Tess. I'll give you a call tomorrow. Andrew's leaving in the morning for about a week. Maybe this Saturday we can all go to the salon for a makeover."

"I'd love that. Thanks for today."

A black SUV pulled curbside behind Tessa's vehicle and Sabina smiled. "I love a man who's punctual for a dinner date."

Andrew hopped out of the back and said, "Where would you like to eat tonight, love? Your wish is my command."

Sabina smiled and said, "Where do you think?"

Chuckling, Andrew walked over to Tessa's car. "And they say women aren't predictable."

"Only Sabina, and only when it comes to cannoli," Tessa said, laughing.

"Uncle Andrew! Hi!" Lydia called from the back seat. He waved and blew her a kiss, which she captured in her hand and applied to her mouth before blowing one back, which he deftly caught.

"I need to get this sleepyhead home to bed. I'll talk to you tomorrow, hon." Tessa rolled up the window, waved, and eased into traffic.

They waved back and Andrew placed his hand in the small of her back as he led her to the SUV.

Neither of them noticed the swirling black mist tailing Tessa's little sports car.

Tell-Tale Publishing would like to thank you for your purchase. If you enjoyed this anthology, please visit our website to find another one, or a full length work by one of its authors.

www.tell-talepublishing.com